Publisher: Valentina Antonia, LLC.

# $OLD

*American Infidel – Book 1*

## by Jaid Black

# Prologue
*Two months earlier*

The U.S. soldier piloting the military aircraft announced they would be landing near Kabul shortly. Dr. Viviana Lincoln took a deep, calming breath. Her destination was usually the same no matter where in the world she was flying to — an undisclosed, Central Intelligence Agency installation. Although a CIA agent in title, she preferred being called by the far less James Bondish "Dr. Lincoln". An expert linguist in several modern and archaic Middle Eastern and North African dialects, Viviana was flown to various government installments in those regions whenever her translation skills were needed. She wasn't an intelligence officer or a spy — just an academic who would have fared well at the Tower of Babel! — so she cringed a bit every time a colleague forgot her preference and referred to her as *Agent* Lincoln.

"We land in fifteen minutes, Agen — Dr. Lincoln."

She glanced up at the co-pilot and smiled. At least he was trying. "Okay thanks." When he kept looking at her quizzically she inwardly sighed, but outwardly answered the question she knew he wanted to ask. She should consider having a card printed out to dispense to anyone who gave her *the look.* "I earned the title 'doctor' twice over so I prefer it to the one supplied to me at work."

He nodded, appeased. Most did.

"Besides, I feel like I should be jumping off high-rises and driving a Lamborghini that morphs into a speedboat when I'm called 'agent'."

He laughed. Again, most did.

Thankfully, he turned back around and did whatever it was co-pilots do. In ten minutes Viviana would be landing in Afghanistan, the one place on earth she'd vowed never to return to. It had been three years since that hellish attack, but she still suffered with nightmares from it. Dr. Berman, the CIA shrink, had ordered her to face her fears—not requested or encouraged her to confront them, but ordered her to. Once commanded, all choice had been removed from the equation, barring her resignation. Had that variable not been in place, the oath to never come back to this Godforsaken land of nightmares would have gladly been kept.

Viviana closed her eyes and rested as comfortably as she could. Military pilots weren't concerned about landing with the same smooth finesse as commercial pilots so they rarely did. This one was proving to be no exception.

Eight minutes — the amount of time she had left before Dr. Berman got his way. She tried to keep her mind clear and present, but it had other plans. It wanted to remember.


*On her belly in a janitorial closet under cleaning supplies, Viviana trembled in the small, dark room as she prayed to God the al Qaeda soldiers didn't find her. The heinous smell of gunpowder, feces, and blood filled the air. It was the odor of human excrement that frightened her most because she knew people released their bowels upon death.*

*"Yalla!" she heard an enemy soldier yell. The precise meaning of "yalla" varied with the dialect, but it usually meant, "let's go" or "come on". She could only hope they were being ordered to evacuate.*

*The door to the closet creaked, inducing Viviana's heartbeat to accelerate. She closed her eyes tightly and prayed she wasn't discovered.*

*"Please don't let them find me," she heard a female voice whimper. "Please God."*

*Viviana's eyes shot open. She recognized that voice. It belonged to Agent Kennedy, an experienced intelligence analyst in her mid-forties. "Marisol?" she whispered.*

*There was a momentary pause. "Vivi?"*

"Yes." She was careful to keep her voice to a barely audible hush. "How many have we lost?"

Asking her colleague questions was apparently not the thing to do. It made Agent Kennedy's breathing labor and her voice rise a bit. "All," Marisol gasped. "A few of the men have been taken as hostages, but most were killed during the initial raid. Kendra, Michaela, and Marie were forced into niqabs and taken who knows where. The other women have all been raped and killed."

Ice-cold fear coursed through Viviana's veins. The females of average or plain appearance had been raped and murdered, while the prettiest ones had either been taken as forced brides or sex slaves. "This isn't happening," she choked out. She and Marisol would likely fall into the latter group of women — a fate literally worse than death to her. "Why haven't we been evac'd yet?"

"I don't think the alarms are working," Marisol said, her breathing thankfully calming. "Vivi — they had an in. I know they did. No other explanation makes a fucking bit of sense!"

There was a traitor in their midst. A scary realization on a normal day — terrifying on this one.

Both of the last remaining women lay on the ground. Viviana stayed hunkered down under cleaning supplies. She thought to tell Marisol to join her when the door was riddled with bullets from a machine gun. Within moments Marisol was screaming as an al Qaeda fighter dragged her from the closet.

*Viviana bit into her hand to keep from sobbing. Her heart slammed in her chest so brutally that she could hear it in her ears. Lying beneath a worn painter's tarp, she could see two more al Qaeda soldiers give the janitorial closet a cursory glance.*

*"All clear," one of them pronounced in a Syrian dialect. He slammed shut what little of the door was left.*

*"Mumtaz," another said, his accent distinctly Saudi.* Excellent.

*Though the door was shut, the bullet holes made seeing through it easy. Shaking and panicked, Viviana continued to bite her hand to keep from accidentally giving herself up.*

*Marisol was stripped of all clothing in front of her very eyes. Viviana's stomach lurched at the thought of watching her colleague get raped. Although she would have laid odds on Marisol falling into the "pretty" group of women, there was no other reason for three men to strip her unless rape was imminent.*

*Agent Kennedy was passed between the smiling men, all of them touching her where they wished to with their hands, but so far none of them undoing their fatigues to take the nightmare further. Marisol had been gagged, but her muffled cries could still be heard, especially when one of the younger men started playing with her nipples.*

*"I take it you desire her," the man she believed to be the trio's leader said to the soldier squeezing one of Marisol's breasts while latching his mouth onto the nipple of the other. It sickened her that*

the leader could speak those words with such levity and humor in his tone. "What is her fate?"

Viviana stilled as she waited to hear what the monster would say. She was glad Marisol couldn't understand Arabic because the conversation they were having about her with the calmness of discussing the weather would have qualified as torture.

The soldier kept sucking, making the other two men laugh. Viviana had never felt so helpless and horrified in her life.

Finally, the soldier's mouth released her nipple with a pop. "I wish to keep her," he said.

Viviana mentally exhaled. There would be no gang rape. Maybe being taken as his wife or concubine was actually the better fate, she told herself. At least then Marisol always had the hope of escape.

"Are you certain?" The leader was rifling through papers. "According to this, she is forty-three years. She may not be able to give you sons."

He shrugged. "I'll take a second wife if she cannot. She is too beautiful not to keep."

The leader nodded. "So be it."

Marisol was quickly clothed in a niqab, a garment that showed only her eyes. Her captor tied her hands together before pressing them against his erection. "This will be inside you tonight," he whispered to her, obviously unconcerned with whether or not she could understand him. "Once you are my wife."

*An eerie silence fell over what was left of the compromised CIA barricade. Only then did Viviana's mind register the fact that the remaining fighters had absconded with Agent Kennedy and were gone.*

*The next several hours passed by in a daze of helplessness and mental disconnect from her body and surroundings. She was afraid to move, too terrified to speak, and could only stare into nothingness. A search and rescue squad finally arrived and located her. They gently pulled her body from under the worn tarp, her hand bleeding from the teeth still piercing it.*

Jarred into awareness by the unsmooth landing, Dr. Lincoln blinked several times in rapid succession. She absently rubbed the hand that still bore a small scar from the stitches it had been given by a triage medic.

"What the fuck?" she heard the co-pilot ask aloud as the plane came to a stop. "What happened here?"

Viviana's eyes widened. She quickly unbuckled her seatbelt and steeled herself for whatever hell was coming.

"They radioed ahead and told me to expect it," the main pilot said. "Some idiot smoked too close to a gas line."

"Shit."

Viviana blew out a breath. They were okay. She could surmise from the back and forth banter that the facility had acquired some damage, but it was nothing to be alarmed about.

"Dr. Lincoln," the pilot said, turning around in his seat, "My orders are to keep you here until a CIA liaison retrieves you."

She nodded. "Sounds good."

"Most of the installation is still completely intact. It's the blockhouses that got fucked."

She frowned thoughtfully. "They must intend to have me live in a safe house and work at the installation." She sighed and glanced away, her gaze absently trailing beyond the tiny window next to her seat. "Great. That won't look suspicious at all," she sardonically muttered.

"I wouldn't worry about it. I would have been given orders to abort and reroute if they didn't have the situation under control."

"I hope you're right," Viviana replied. She closed her eyes. "I really do."

# Chapter One

*Wazir Akbar Khan:*
*Northern Kabul, Afghanistan*

"The top ten signs you are getting too old for this shit are…"

Viviana smiled. She loved hearing the laughter of her colleagues, which was the reason she came up with new top ten list countdowns à la David Letterman on a near daily basis. That and the fact it helped take her mind off how boring it was in the CIA safe house.

For the past two months she had been acting as a translator between interrogators and their jihadist prisoners. All day long she sat in boring, sensory deprived interrogation cells only to return "home" to a boring, sensory deprived safe house. Simply put, it was too risky to leave the walled shelter these days. If an American hostage was a jihadist's dream come true, an American employed by the U.S. government was the wet, nocturnal version of it. It was a reality she knew firsthand all too well.

Not that she was complaining about the lack of chaos and drama—quite the opposite. Dr. Lincoln would take boredom over strife any day of the week.

Viviana shared the estate with four soldiers and two cyber-analysts. When they left the compound they did so as a pretend family, keeping up the illusion via native dress and customs that their household consisted of two brothers and their obedient wives. On the upside, she only had to get into character long enough to enter and exit the CIA installation. On the downside, it was the only movement she'd had in over eight weeks.

"Number ten," Viviana said as Corporal John Williams put her dinner in front of her. "Oh thanks, John. Looks good!"

Her "husband" grinned as he sat at the table with the rest of their make-believe family. John couldn't have been older than twenty-five so she constantly teased him that he must be a cougar-lover if he'd "married" a thirty-six-year-old such as herself. He'd let her know in no uncertain terms he was more than willing to go there for real, but Viviana just couldn't see herself with a guy that young. The mere thought made her feel like a creeper.

"You were saying?" Corporal Williams asked.

Viviana nodded. "Not that our sperm of a husband is old enough to be too old for anything, but the number ten sign you are getting too old for this shit is…"

Everyone at the table laughed. They loved this game—and teasing John—as much as she did.

"You can no longer tell if you're hot because of the climate or because you're going menopausal," Viviana stated, grinning.

Boisterous amusement ensued. "You aren't old enough for that either, Vivi," husband number two, Analyst Majid Khan, laughed. "But it would explain the bitchiness if you were."

"Boom!" She clapped her hands and chuckled at the American born Muslim of Afghan descent. "Okay your turn, smart ass!"

Majid never passed on his turn. He was as quick-witted and humorous as she was. "The number nine sign you are getting too old for this shit," he returned, "is when you nod off during an air raid."

Viviana slapped her hand on the table. She laughed as hard as the rest of their little family. By the time they reached number one on that night's top ten, there wasn't a dry eye in the dining room. They poured wine, toasted each other, and happily consumed their dinner together.

"It's my turn to cook tomorrow," Viviana reminded the group. She grinned. "I know everyone *loooooves* Vivi's cooking night!"

"Oh fuck me," John moaned. "I'll start taking an antibiotic now."

* * * * *

"Sorry I'm late," Viviana said to Agent Bill Cosgrove as she removed her niqab and cloak. Now wearing only black suit pants and a simple but classy white, silk shirt, she ran a hand through her wild mane of dark blonde curls. Her turquoise eyes sparkled as she smiled at the interrogator she'd been assigned to today. She didn't particularly care for Cosgrove on a personal level, but she always strove to keep things professional and cordial. "Corporal Williams drove today. Need I say more?"

"No," Bill returned. "That explanation covers everything."

"He kept yelling at the camels." She sighed. "I'm pretty sure they didn't give a shit."

The agent handed her a cup of coffee and a folder. "We landed a big fish, Viviana."

She quirked an eyebrow. "Dolphin? Shark?"

"Try a blue whale."

Her eyes widened. "Wow. That major of a player?"

Bill nodded. "Muhammad al-Jihad al-Raqqah. Number two on the FBI's Most Wanted, second only to the self-proclaimed caliph himself."

"Fuck me," Viviana murmured. She shook her head. "I'm assuming I don't need to put the niqab back on before we go in?"

"Nope. That monster will never see the light of day. You don't have to worry about being recognized."

She nodded. "You sure he doesn't speak English?"

He frowned. "Ninety-nine percent sure."

Viviana sighed. "If he's never getting out it doesn't matter anyway. I just thought I'd ask. Force of habit."

Agent Cosgrove said nothing to that. He was too socially awkward, amongst other things, to tolerate in long doses.

"You ready?" he asked.

"Can I bring in my coffee?"

"Yeah. He's handcuffed."

"Then I'm ready."

They walked down a long stone corridor until they reached the cell. Agent Cosgrove nodded to a soldier who stood guard at the interrogation room currently housing al-

Raqqah. The soldier turned the key, opened the door, and waited for Viviana and Cosgrove to walk inside. Once they were in, she heard the door close and the key turn, locking them in.

This was so routine Viviana didn't even bother to glance at the prisoner as she took one of the seats opposite him at the table. She sipped on her coffee while flipping through the folder of notes Agent Cosgrove had given her. Without looking up, she introduced herself in Arabic to al-Raqqah.

"My name is Dr. Viviana Lincoln." She saw no reason to lie about her name. Translators weren't exactly hot targets to the jihadi cells. "I'm only a linguist, not an interrogator. Will you speak to a woman or would you prefer to wait until a male translator is available...however long that might take?"

She reverted to English. "Can we get some air in here, agent? And preferably some food." She continued browsing through the notes.

"Yeah," Cosgrove told her. He banged twice on the door. "I'll be right back."

"Will you speak to a woman?" Viviana asked again in Arabic. She blew out a breath as she rifled through his rap sheet. He definitely would never see the light of day again. "Will you speak to a woman?"

"Naam."

Naam — *Yes.*

Viviana finally glanced up. She stilled. Her breathing hitched as her gaze flicked over his face. "What the fuck did they do to you?" she rhetorically murmured in English.

Muhammad al-Jihad al-Raqqah had been tortured so badly as to be unrecognizable. She wouldn't have been able to tell what he looked like had she not been holding a photo of him in her hand. The forty-year-old jihadist was handsome as demons go. Or at least he had been.

Viviana started feeling nauseous. One of his eyes was swollen shut, the other lacerated and purple with bruises. What looked to be lashes from a whip had cut up his face, some of the wounds still seeping. Remnants of a beard that looked to have been painfully yanked out in patches matted into deep gashes. She lifted a shaky hand to her mouth. This had never been part of her contract.

"Air's on high and danishes are in my hand," Cosgrove said as the door closed and locked behind him. "Will he speak to a woman?"

"Yes." She craned her neck to look at Cosgrove. "But this woman won't be speaking to him. What the fuck, agent?" Angry or not, Viviana was careful not to use his name in front

17

of the prisoner. Unlike translators, interrogators were high on retribution lists. "I do not translate in situations like this and you damn well know it!"

"I know," Cosgrove said. He sighed and set the danishes down in front of her. "They insisted on a translator with security clearance though and you—"

She held up a palm. "Do you really think I can eat something that resembles the oozing, pus-filled slashes on his face?"

"Doctor, can we please get on with this?"

Viviana blinked. "I just said I'm not doing this. I do not agree with tactics like this used on anyone and I won't help." She set down her coffee and splayed her hands. "Period, the end."

Cosgrove's face turned red. "I'll make sure you never translate for another camel fucker in your life if you keep this up!"

Her green-blue eyes narrowed. "How. Dare. You." Her back stiffened. "Even if you wielded such clout, which you don't, I won't take part in this."

He ran a hand through his balding hair. "We shouldn't be talking in front of him on the off-chance he knows English, but fuck it at this point." He grunted. "What do I have to do to get your compliance?"

Viviana glanced back at the prisoner. The one eye he could see out of was trained on her. She swallowed against the bile in her throat. She wasn't an eye for an eye type of person. She loathed this barbaric warlord who was responsible for the deaths of so many Americans, but what the CIA had done to al-Raqqah was making her feel sorry for him—the last emotion on earth she wanted to feel towards a terrorist.

"Attend to his wounds," she murmured, looking at Cosgrove. "Feed him and hydrate him. Those are my terms or I walk."

"Women," the agent muttered.

Viviana's eyebrows rose. "You're really pressing your luck with me, agent. I don't need this low-paying ass job. I do it out of patriotism, I do it because my parents were killed in one of their suicide bombings, but your mouth is this close to ensuring I turn in my resignation. I never wanted to come back to this fucked up country anyway."

"Fine." Cosgrove stood up and walked to the door. He banged on it twice. "Just don't get pissy with me if we're here all night because you had to waste time on this filth!"

"Whatever," she said to Cosgrove before looking back at the prisoner. "They are bringing in someone from medical to dress your wounds before we begin," she told al-Raqqah in Arabic. "You will also be given food and water."

"Shukran." *Thank you.*

Viviana begrudgingly inclined her head. Her kindness to him would only extend so far and that limit had been reached. If this terrorist turned out to be the one responsible for the suicide bombing in Kenya that had killed her vacationing parents, God help them both. He wouldn't need food, water, and medical care because she'd kill him with her bare hands.

She resumed reading the contents of the folder, but could feel his gaze homed in on her. It was disconcerting to sit this close to a sadistic mass-murderer. She'd never translated for a major player before. She decided she didn't like it.

"I prefer the blue," al-Raqqah muttered in Arabic. "See all that is mine."

Viviana glanced up. One of her eyebrows rose. "Are you feeling all right?" The eye he could see out of never strayed from her. It would have been unnerving if she hadn't known he was broaching hallucinatory. His nonsensical words underlined that fact.

"Naam." *Yes.*

She nodded and resumed reading. That fucking Cosgrove needed to get a move on already.

* * * * *

It had been a long day. Viviana was relieved she'd showered before work because by the time she returned to the safe house and made dinner she was too exhausted to do anything beyond peel off her clothes and plop into bed. Wearing nothing but see-through lingerie, she laid down with a weary groan.

She didn't know why she wore lingerie under her clothes every day in Afghanistan because she never bothered donning it for lovers, much less herself, back home. She supposed it was her small way of bucking the system of female oppression and expression that weighed down her soul whenever work required her presence in the region. There was power in symbolism—even if only she knew about it.

Viviana's thoughts drifted back to Muhammad al-Jihad al-Raqqah. After he'd been cleaned up, fed, and hydrated, his wounds had looked less severe. Painful, no doubt, but not life-threatening. Regardless, she wasn't looking forward to spending tomorrow translating between the interrogator and the terrorist yet again. There was something in al-Raqqah's sharp gaze that sent chills down her spine. A knowing. A promise. A—

She sighed. She couldn't put her finger on it. She only knew it didn't set well with her.

*"I prefer the blue. See all that is mine."*

Viviana realized he hadn't been altogether with it when he'd uttered those cryptic words, but they haunted her nonetheless. Despite his injuries, that hawk-like gaze of his had never waned in its intensity. Nor had it strayed from her even once.

She absently looked at the ceiling as she blew out a breath. She did a double take. Curious, she turned on the light and squinted at the ceiling. There was something up there she hadn't noticed before. She wouldn't have noticed it tonight if a moonbeam hadn't reflected on it in a weird way.

Viviana stilled. Her eyes widened and her pulse quickened. "It's a camera," she rasped.

She jumped out of bed and prepared to get dressed. Her image in the mirror stopped her cold.

*"I prefer the blue. See all that is mine."*

Oh. My. God.

Her breathing labored as she stared at her reflection. Blue. Her lingerie, the only see-through pair she owned, was blue.

"This is so not good," she unsteadily muttered to herself. She threw on a t-shirt and the closest pair of yoga pants. She had to get downstairs and alert everyone *now*. She might have been a translator and not an agent, but it didn't take a trained eye to realize their safe house had been compromised. It might never have been safe at all. "Shit, shit, shit!"

The sound of machine guns and screams shattered the tranquility of the night. Viviana's heart slammed in her chest. Wild-eyed with terror, she didn't know what to do. She could hear return fire coming from below, quickly followed by more machine guns. A sickly, eerie silence followed.

She covered her mouth to keep from screaming and slumped to the floor. Her teeth sank into one hand, the raid from three years past having auto-programmed that coping mechanism into her. She didn't know which side had won, but clearly there was a victor. Her question would be answered all too soon.

"The sheikh wants her alive!" she heard a man shout in Arabic. "Take her, but look upon her only as much as necessary!"

Viviana's hysteria mandated screaming, but she kept her teeth sunk into her hand to stop herself from giving into the urge. Who was the sheikh? Which of them did he want alive?

*Why* did he want any of the women here? What happened to the ones he didn't want? Would it be like three years ago, all of them raped and executed?

Her bedroom door made a sickening cracking sound as it was kicked in. Her hands flew from her mouth to the floor as she instinctually scooted back. A man burst inside, wearing what appeared to be a gas mask. Viviana screamed. He rolled a smoking ball toward her. Her mind, broken from fear, wondered if it was a grenade, but she wasn't given time to contemplate it.

Gas spewed out from the ball, forcing her to choke. She gasped for breath, but there was none to be had. Viviana could feel herself losing consciousness as she fell on her side. It was the last thought she'd ever have as a free woman.

# Chapter Two

Viviana spent what felt like several days floating in and out of consciousness. Very little made sense in this hazy, woozy state she'd been consigned to. She knew she was in a room, she comprehended she was lying on a bed, and she had vague, scattered recollections of women's faces hovering over her. That was the extent of her knowledge.

*Am I in a hospital? Was I rescued?*

She didn't know. Every time she tried to open her eyes for more than a few seconds she was rewarded with another jolt of searing pain.

*Think, Vivi. Surely you remember something…*

Quick, barely coherent images flashed through her mind's eye:

Being sponge bathed by a woman in hijab. Another woman, also wearing a headscarf, forcing her to drink some sort of broth. An IV in her arm. A man looming over her, telling her he was feeding some manner of medicine into the IV.

Medicine. Yes, Viviana remembered him calling it medicine. She hadn't been able to see him, only hear him and smell his scent. He had definitely been real though, most likely a doctor. He had taken delicate care of her, forging a connection in her fevered mind between comfort and his male scent. Yes, he had to be a doctor. The thought instilled hope in her.

Blinking several times in rapid succession, she attempted to regain her visual acuity. She whimpered as she did so, the strain causing her head to pound and her belly to churn with nausea. Her consciousness was coming back though so she was determined to see clearly no matter how much she ached in the doing.

"Do not injure yourself," a male voice murmured in thickly accented English. "You will feel much improved by tomorrow."

Viviana groaned and closed her eyes. She remembered that voice. She swallowed as she tried to find hers. "Doctor," she said hoarsely. Her head turned on the pillow. Her throat was too dry and scratchy. "Water," she managed to rasp out. "Please."

She could smell his comforting scent before she felt his large hand cradle the back of her head. He lifted a cup to her lips. Yes, it was the same physician who'd been attending to her.

"Take only enough to wet your mouth," he instructed in a calm, patient tone. His voice was deep, familiar. She supposed her subconscious recognized his distinct timbre from the time she'd unknowingly spent in his care. "I do not wish for you to be in pain."

Viviana did as ordered, which turned out to be a good thing. The water felt like heaven to her dry mouth and parched lips, but burned like hell as it trickled down her raw throat. He made to remove the cup, but she weakly touched his hand. "More. Please."

It took several minutes, but they repeated the action three more times. By the fourth sip, her throat stung less, even if it was still raw. Exhausted from her efforts, she was grateful when he gently laid her head back on the pillow.

"Please." Forming words was tiring, but she didn't want him to leave. "Stay."

She could sense him hesitate. He probably had other patients to tend to.

"Please," Viviana said weakly. She found his hand. "Don't leave me alone."

Images from her last night in the safe house flashed through her mind. Machine guns. Return fire. Helpless screams. Her door being kicked in...

She whimpered. Tears gathered in her closed eyes. The doctor tightened his hold on her hand.

"They will rape or kill me," she whispered.

Again, she could sense him hesitate. "No one will bring harm to you," he finally murmured.

The act of speaking was slowly getting easier, yet exponentially more tiring. Viviana knew she was about to pass out so it was important the physician understood she was a target. "They murdered my parents. My colleagues. I am next."

She could feel the doctor's reassuring hand clasping hers. Succumbing to the exhaustion that enveloped her, she fell into oblivious sleep.

\* \* \* \* \*

Sheikh Muhammad al-Jihad al-Raqqah stared at his sleeping captive. Even in slumber her hand still clung to his — something he realized she'd never do once awake and cognizant of whom her precious "doctor" was. That, he knew, would take much time and patience.

Dr. Viviana Lincoln was a learned, Western woman. The customs and culture of his people would be difficult at best for such a female to accept. But *inshallah* — God willing — she would eventually. At least he hoped so…for both their sakes.

Muhammad had been watching her for two months, long before his capture and escape from infidel clutches. At first, he had felt nothing but lust for her. The nights in her bedroom when she would play with her nipples and rub her clit, masturbating herself into oblivion...

Never had he wanted to fuck a woman more. The need had been so powerful that he'd committed the same *haram* — forbidden — act as she by masturbating as he watched her touch herself. A pious man should always relieve himself inside his wife, not his hand, but a drone strike had killed both his wives two years past. That same air raid had also taken his children from him — a fact he tried not to think about lest grief and fury take root again.

After several days of watching Viviana in real-time through the crystal-clear cameras installed in the CIA safe house, his lust had turned into a peculiar mixture of admiration and enjoyment tinged with obsession. The lust never wavered of course, but Muhammad had gotten to see all the various facets of her complex personality. Who she was while in the company of colleagues, who she was when alone in her bedroom, her sense of humor, her compassionate nature, and her steadfast belief she was on — as she herself called it — the right side of history.

It was the latter part he had an issue with.

Her people had tried to break him; they had not succeeded. His physical wounds would heal, save a scar or two on his face and back, but he had not succumbed to weakness and divulged any information to his brutal captors that he didn't wish for them to know.

Muhammad stared down at the beautiful, sleeping American still clutching his hand. He ran the fingers of his free hand through her cascading mane of dark gold curls.

Tomorrow would be different. Tomorrow Viviana would be recovered enough to realize who he was.

He sighed. He had a lot of work ahead of him.

# Chapter Three

Viviana awoke with a groan. Much of the pain was gone, though not all of it. Still, the doctor had been correct — she did feel much improved today. Of course, she hadn't tried to open her eyes yet either. Whatever type of gas that had been used to render her unconscious had certainly done a number on her eyes. She vaguely recalled the two women in hijab washing them out several times. She'd cried from the pain.

Blinking several times to adjust her vision, Viviana let out a sigh of relief when she was able to open them without intense, jarring pain searing through her skull. She hadn't gone blind or lost any visual acuity at all. She was a bit dizzy, still a little woozy, but all in all she felt a thousand times better.

Slowly, very slowly, she brought herself into an upright position in the bed. The soft blanket covering her body fell to her waist. It was only then, when the chill from the air conditioning caused her nipples to stiffen, Viviana realized she was completely naked.

Her forehead crinkled. She decided she must have been recuperating in an incredibly liberal Afghan hospital. Nudity wasn't the norm for patients, especially females, in the Middle East. Hell, it wasn't even the norm for American hospitals!

Maybe this facility had run out of those bed gowns that open in the back.

Viviana eyed her surroundings. She'd never seen such a palatial hospital room, let alone such a posh one. The opulence was a bit overwhelming. Moroccan tile floors, a huge Persian rug that easily would have sold for over a hundred grand back home, mosaics and fine art on the walls, a lavish body of water that was either a bathtub or a swimming pool...

She blinked. This made no sense.

Naked or not, Viviana wanted to have a look around. She hoped her legs were steady enough to keep her on her feet. Turning herself to the right side of the hospital bed, she stood up, albeit shakily. That's when she noticed the IV in her arm. She visually scanned the room for a cart to hook the IV onto so she could walk around with it.

"Damn," she muttered. "Nothing."

She coughed, her throat scratchy. At least there was a pitcher of water and a single glass on the table next to the bed. There was also a remote to what Viviana presumed was a television. Now if she could find the television said remote went to, she'd at least have something to occupy her time until the doctor or one of the nurses returned to check on her. She glanced around, but saw nothing. Sighing, she next looked for the nurse's call button. No luck there either.

Disgruntled, Viviana poured herself a glass of water, grabbed the remote, and made herself comfortable in the bed again. The typeset below each button on the remote was in Arabic so she searched for the button with the word that meant "power" beneath it. "There you are." She coughed again. Deciding to wet her throat before continuing her inspection of the remote, she slowly sipped water from the glass before setting it back on the table next to her. Much better.

She didn't know why she was fiddling with a remote to a non-existent television, but clicked the power button anyway. She gasped when a hidden compartment opened from the ceiling and a huge LCD screen came down and backed up to the perfect height and distance from her. She smiled. She was definitely praising this hospital on the comment cards they typically left behind.

The television roared to life. Viviana quickly lowered the volume. The channel was already set to the local Al Jazeera news affiliate, which was precisely what she'd wanted. As much trepidation as she felt concerning the answer to the question of what had become of the safe house's other inhabitants, she needed to know. She picked up her water and sat back as she watched the broadcast. It didn't take long to be brought up to speed.

*"It's been four days since the American government's safe house in the northern Kabul suburb of Wazir Akbar Khan was raided by insurgents. The attack left six of the house's seven American occupants dead, including four U.S. military and two CIA intelligence analysts. We go to our Afghan correspondent Nazir al-Raja for the latest developments in this story. Nazir..."*

Viviana closed her eyes and took a deep breath. Her gut intuition had already told her what Al Jazeera TV just confirmed: she was the sole survivor. It was three years ago all over again. John, Majid, Belinda—all of them—*gone*. She wanted to cry, but was too depleted for even that. She might not have been besties with any of her colleagues, but they were good people. Nobody deserved to die in such a heinous manner, least of all them. She opened her eyes, her haunted gaze absently flicking back to the television.

*"...The whereabouts of the seventh are still unknown."*

Viviana frowned. She, the seventh, was here in the hospital. Had the CIA lied to the media in order to keep the terrorists guessing? The thought sent a surge of relief through her entire body even as a photograph of her face flashed onto the screen.

*"Agent Viviana Lincoln, a linguist and translator for the American government, has been missing since the attack. A video just released by the so-called Islamic State, in which the group claims responsibility for taking the American female hostage, appears to show Dr. Lincoln being treated for her wounds at an undisclosed location somewhere deep within the Daesh stronghold of Syria. The American government has yet to comment, stating only that they are in the process of authenticating the video."*

She stilled. Grainy footage of her lying in the bed she currently occupied filled the screen. Her pulse sped as her heart slammed in her chest.

"Oh my God," Viviana whispered, her stare unblinking. Chills racked her body. "This can't be happening."

Memories of the attack flooded her awareness. The sounds, the smells, the terror she'd experienced...and the words she'd heard shouted.

*"The sheikh wants her alive! Take her, but look upon her only as much as necessary!"*

Viviana was the *her* this sheikh wanted? Her breathing grew increasingly labored as dozens of competing but equally horrific scenarios raced through her mind. Rape, torture, a public beheading...all of the above? She had escaped those hells three years ago. The odds of escaping at least one of those outcomes a second time couldn't be in her favor.

35

"No wonder they kept me naked," she said shakily. "They think I won't run."

It was a bet they would lose.

Tearing the IV out of her arm, Viviana paid no attention to the pain or to the blood dripping from the minor wound she'd just caused herself. The only thing she could concentrate on was getting out of wherever in the hell she was and running like an Olympic sprinter to anywhere but here. Hopefully a sympathetic person, or at least a drone, would spot her. She prayed she would find something—anything—that could double as clothing, but already knew she wouldn't let nudity stop her.

She glanced at the blanket. No, it was too bulky and heavy. It would only weigh her down.

Footsteps were coming. Her eyes widened. She jumped off the bed and onto feet being ill supported by unsteady legs. She'd forgotten how weak her legs were likely to be!

Realizing that in her current condition she couldn't outrun whoever was coming, Viviana picked up the pitcher of water, emptied its contents on the floor, and wobbled towards the door. She stood behind it, wide-eyed and heart racing, preparing to hurl the urn at the first person who entered.

The door opened. She raised the pitcher.

A man entered. He glanced at the empty bed before running toward it.

Viviana launched the urn, aiming for his head. She missed. He spun around as the pitcher shattered against the wall behind him.

She didn't bother looking at her captor as she fled to the other side of the door, slammed it behind her, and ran as fast as two shaky legs could go. Her heart was pounding in her ears, her lungs on fire from being overworked too soon, but she ran down the long corridor anyway. She could hear the man shouting at her and cursing in Arabic as he gave chase, but she paid his words little heed. Her only thought was freedom, her only objective to make it outside and onto the street.

At the end of the corridor was another set of doors. Gasping for breath, Viviana tried to thrust them open, but they were locked. She started pounding on the doors while screaming for help, even though she realized nobody on the other side of it was likely to aid her in any way.

She could sense that the man was directly behind her, watching, no doubt amused by her feeble attempt at escape. Facing the door, she sank down onto the floor and started to cry, her head bowed and her naked body balled up. "Somebody help me," she weakly gasped. "Please."

"I told you not to injure yourself," the man said in his tongue. "We must work on your listening skills."

She recognized the voice—and his musky scent. It was the doctor.

"Please help me leave, doctor," Viviana said feebly. She raised her head, tears streaming down her cheeks as she finally looked at him. "Please. I don't want—"

The world seemed to spin out of control as Viviana stared with rounded eyes at the doctor who was no doctor. Her pulse immediately skyrocketed, making her feel dizzy and her surroundings surreal.

She knew that face. His matted beard had been shaved off, leaving nothing but a five o'clock shadow. His astute brown gaze was as homed in on her now as it had been in the interrogation room. The swelling around his left eye had subsided, the only reminder of its former presence there a lingering bruise and a small cut.

Muhammad al-Jihad al-Raqqah.

*"I prefer the blue. See all that is mine."*

The FBI's most wanted. The mass murderer of innocent people. The closest confidant of the self-heralded caliph.

*"I prefer the blue. See all that is mine."*

"Oh my God." Viviana swallowed roughly, her aqua eyes shedding fresh tears. Suddenly it all made sense. *"Nooooooo!"*

* * * * *

Muhammad carried Viviana back to his bedroom like a kicking, screaming—and bleeding—sack of potatoes. She was stronger than she looked, but still no match for his 6′4″ height and heavily muscled build.

"Enough," he said sternly. He used his free hand to spank her one sharp time on the bare ass. "You will injure yourself."

She simultaneously gasped in outrage and cried in faux pain. "I'd rather die my way than whatever you have planned for me!"

Viviana pummeled his back with her fists. He sighed. He didn't want to hurt her pride by informing her he owned massage chairs that dealt harder blows.

"Do you need another spanking?" he asked, purposely raising his voice. "Stop this before you bleed worse from that open wound on your arm."

"I'm not a child! You have no right to spank me!"

He grunted. "You behave as one." He opened the doors to his private suite and carried her inside. "So I treat you as one."

39

Muhammad decided he might as well get the next part over and done with. "And I do have the right."

He could hear her jaw tighten simply by the way she enunciated her words. "By whose authority?" she ground out.

"Allah's." *God's.*

Muhammad carefully placed her on the bed. Viviana quickly picked up the blanket and held it up to shield her nakedness. He quirked an eyebrow.

"Show me your arm," he commanded.

"Why?"

"Show!"

He might have spoken a bit too gruffly. Her eyes widened, the fear she harbored towards him apparent. Nevertheless, it worked, so he'd deal with one task at a time. Grabbing a fresh hand cloth and dipping it into the bowl of clean water she *hadn't* emptied on the floor, he sat next to her on the bed and gently tended to the wound she'd dealt herself by ripping the IV out of her arm.

"Why do you care about that stupid puncture?" Viviana asked. Her voice was steady, but he picked up on the underlying, barely noticeable tremble to it. "It makes no sense to clean me up only to kill me."

"I'm not killing you," he responded without looking at her.

For some odd reason that admission made her breathing grow heavier and her pulse accelerate. He would quickly learn why.

"Are you selling me?" she breathed out. She stammered a bit. "Please just tell me what I'm facing."

Muhammad reached in the drawer of the nightstand for a bandage and medical tape. He wrapped her arm at the elbow, bit off a chunk of adhesive, and taped the bandage shut. That accomplished, he gave her his full attention—something he shouldn't have done. His cock grew painfully stiff just gazing into her rounded eyes. God had tinted their color to a beautiful, unique green-blue. He shifted uncomfortably.

"Are you selling me?" Viviana asked quietly.

"No. I am not."

She gulped. "Really?"

"Wallah." *I swear to God.*

Her teeth sank into her lower lip. He could tell she was confused.

"Am I being used in a hostage trade?" she asked.

"Laa." *No.*

She blinked. "Then what?"

He decided it would be best to just put the truth to her and give her some time to come to terms with it. Muhammad's firm gaze clashed with her frightened one.

"You will not be killed, maimed, used as a bargaining chip, sold, or otherwise humiliated. You showed me kindness and I do not repay such acts by committing monstrosities against such a person."

Her eyes glittered with hope for the first time. "You're letting me go home?"

Muhammad kept his words steady and deliberate. "You *are* home."

Her jaw dropped a bit. She quickly closed it then shook her head as if to clear it. "I don't understand…"

"You belong to me now," he said matter-of-factly. "Kilik ele." *All of you is mine.*

He should have been offended by how close she looked to fainting, but he was too focused to think on it.

"No." Viviana shook her head. "I—no. That really won't work out."

"It has already worked out. You are American no more, you are Dr. Viviana Lincoln no more."

She opened her mouth to speak, but no words came out. He seized the moment, wanting to finish the conversation. His erection was starting to drip pre-cum so it was best if he left his — their — apartments for the moment.

"You are now Sheikha Viviana al-Raqqah, my bride."

A myriad of emotions crossed her face, none of them particularly welcomed. Stunned disbelief, outrage, horror, terror — she was feeling the full impact, realizing what he actually did have in store for her.

Her sparkly eyes narrowed. "I will never marry you. Kill me now!" she said grandly. "I will *never* say yes!"

Muhammad's pride smarted a bit, but he was wise enough to place himself in her position. She believed him to be a sadistic monster. Even in the absence of fear, Viviana had not been raised to be meek, demur, and submissive, but to hold the same station in life as a man. Truth be told, her independent spirit was part of her allure.

"I said you *are* my bride," he murmured, "not you *will be* my bride."

Her breathing hitched and grew heavy again. "No," she rasped. "That isn't possible." Her gaze took on a wild look, much like a tigress that'd been cornered by a hunter. "I would have remembered something like *that* no matter how out of it I was."

"You were never a part of the ceremony."

She frowned. "That's sort of a requirement!"

"In your world perhaps, not in mine."

Her expression became desperate. "You can't do this! I *refuuuuse* to accept this!"

"We are married now." His nostrils flared as he stood up and slashed an unforgiving hand through the air. "It is done."

"How? I never gave my consent. Consent of the bride is required in Islam!" Viviana realized she sounded as hysterical as she felt. She clutched onto her knowledge of Sharia law like a talisman. "I know my rights!"

Was that amusement in his gaze? She wanted to jab those brown eyes of his right out of their sockets.

"Consent from her *wali* also suffices."

"I don't have a guardian!"

He shrugged. "You were appointed one."

"Who?"

"The local *qadi*."

A judge. Well wasn't that sooooo convenient!

"I want to speak to the *qadi*—my *wali*," she franticly demanded. "Now."

He made a mocking tsk-tsk sound. "Certainly my beautiful, educated bride knows that her husband becomes her guardian upon marriage?" His expression hardened. "You are speaking to your one and only *wali* already."

Fury enveloped her. "You managed to get a *qadi* to act as the *wali* of an American hostage?" Viviana released the blanket and threw her hands in the air. Fuck being naked. She no longer cared. "Wait until my government finds out about this bullshit!"

Muhammad was silent for a long moment. His gaze lingered at her naked breasts before returning to her face. "Do you honestly believe they don't already know?" he murmured.

Her eyes widened. A chill of foreboding traveled down the length of her spine. "They don't know," she rasped. She swallowed against the lump in her throat. "They wouldn't do that."

Not even Viviana believed the words she was weakly uttering. Unless the hostage in question was an elected official with visibility or someone equally high profile, pretty much everybody and anybody else was viewed as collateral damage for the right price. In that way, her government was no different than the devil it chased.

"What was I worth?" she asked quietly. "Some oil? A fucking camel?" The fight went completely out of her as the truth settled in. "Or nothing at all?"

His expression softened. "Excessively valuable information. Let us just say you have commanded the highest bride-price in the history of my people."

She wished that made her feel better. "So who am I now?" she asked dispassionately. "Wife number ten thousand and two?"

He didn't smile, but she could see the amusement twinkling in his eyes again. Damn him.

"You are well aware a Muslim man can have but four wives," Muhammad said drolly.

"*Only* four. Oh joy." Viviana pulled the blanket up, once again concealing her breasts. She flopped back onto the pillows and stared at the ceiling. "Just call me 'Four' then, like the guy in *Divergent*. Might as well tattoo it on my forehead while you're at it."

"You are my only wife."

She rolled her eyes. "I'm not going to pretend to be an expert on you because I'm just a linguist, not an intel agent, but I do know you have at least two wives and three sons."

He was quiet for a long moment. She started to wonder if he was just ignoring her now.

"Had," he finally said.

"Huh?"

"I *had* two wives and three sons. Past tense."

She came up on her elbows and crooked her neck to look at him. "What do you mean?"

His jaw steeled, but Viviana didn't glance away. She wanted to know what he was talking about.

"They were murdered in a drone strike two years ago," Muhammad finally answered. "A U.S. drone strike."

Her gaze softened. "I'm sorry," she whispered.

Muhammad was apparently not one to accept pity. His demeanor became aloof and somewhat cold.

"Bathe yourself," he instructed her, walking toward the egresses. "I'll be back in a few hours to consummate our marriage." He came to a halt as he reached the doors. He turned around, his gaze clashing with hers. "For the record, I am not responsible for the death of your parents and do not know who is."

Viviana's pulse raced at the mere mention of her dead family. She said nothing, only stared.

"But we do know who killed my sons," Muhammad muttered. He blinked, as if forcing the memories away. "Be prepared before I return. I will send in my mother and sister to aid you."

Viviana blushed. She knew what *prepared* meant in this culture. All her hair, save her eyebrows and what was on her head, would be removed in a process called sugaring. It was similar to waxing, but allegedly much more painful.

"They took from me three children." Muhammad opened the doors before crooking his neck to look at her from over his shoulder. "So you will give to me six."

She swallowed. His eyebrows rose.

"Three hours," he commanded. "Be prepared."

# Chapter Four

Sheikha Viviana al-Raqqah. Holy fucking shit.

It would have been less shocking to discover Elvis really was still alive and the moon was nothing more than a ball of Swiss cheese. Of all the *it-could-happen* outcomes she'd had to steel herself for as possible consequences of working for the CIA on hostile terrain, this particular scenario had never factored into her thinking.

What if he was telling the truth? What if her government truly did know she was now the forced bride of a jihadist? She grimly decided the only good point to this was Muhammad would probably kill himself off eventually in some suicide bombing or another. She just hoped it wasn't while anywhere near *her*.

"Bride of Jihad," she muttered to herself. "Bride of Chucky is more appealing!" At least a possessed doll could be thrown into a fireplace.

Viviana rubbed her aching temples. She didn't want to bathe, she didn't want sugared, and she damn sure didn't want to consummate this farce of a marriage. She knew a handful of CIA operatives, male and female alike, who had done this sort of thing before. The major difference being they were given a choice. That and the fact they were "taking one for the team" as undercover agents who knew they'd eventually get out.

She couldn't help but wonder just what kind of intelligence had been traded in exchange for her lifetime imprisonment. If she had a way to upload a video to YouTube telling the world what the CIA had done to her she—

Viviana stilled. She frowned thoughtfully.

A cursory glance around the bedroom alone bespoke of an owner who kept up to date on technology. Given that knowledge, the YouTube idea wasn't exactly farfetched.

Her teeth sank into her lower lip as she mulled over the possibilities. Perhaps all hope was not yet lost.

\* \* \* \* \*

"I can do this myself," Viviana said awkwardly. Her cheeks pinkened. "Wallah." *I swear to God.*

Muhammad's mother was unconvinced and flatly told her so. "Lazem osa'e feke Bl awal," she ground out. *You must earn my trust.* "Ana ma aa'ate el se'ea la hadan gherek." *I do not give it freely to one such as yourself.*

Viviana frowned. As if she wanted to be here any more than the older woman wanted her here.

"Ummi!" her companion chastised, embarrassed. She was obviously Muhammad's sister for *ummi* meant *mom* or *mommy*. "Momo asked us to be kind," she whispered. "Respect his wishes, please."

Viviana glanced up at her so-called husband's younger sibling. She was a pretty girl, most likely in her early twenties. Her eyes were gentle, kind.

"Bah!" the mother-in-law she already loathed spat. "Her kind killed your brothers—my sons! They murdered my grandsons in cold blood as well as their mothers!"

"Excuse me," Viviana cut in. Freshly bathed by force, she now sat on the bed naked, her hands covering as much of her large breasts as they could. "Let's recall I do speak Arabic," she said in Arabic.

"I have not forgotten, infidel."

"*Ummi*," her daughter said more forcefully, "enough."

Viviana pasted on a blatantly fake smile. "You know how to make a hostage bride feel welcomed. I'm looking forward to spending the holidays with you already."

Both women's faces turned red—the younger from embarrassment, the elder from anger.

"Listen to me, *kafir*," Muhammad's mother bit out. *Kafir* was a derogatory term for a non-Muslim. "I put up with you in my home for the sake of my son only. Do not push me."

"Then help me escape," Viviana said evenly. Her gaze narrowed. "I put up with you because I have no choice at the moment. Give me clothes and an open door and I'll do us both a favor."

She waved that away. "You would be killed long before you reached the Syrian border, much less your embassy."

"That would be my problem, not yours."

"We should not be discussing these things," her daughter interjected. "Momo will not be pleased."

"Aaliyah," the older woman said. She took a deep breath and exhaled slowly. "I am trying."

Viviana's eyebrows rose. If this was trying she'd hate to see her *not* try.

"Momo has told me things of your new daughter-in-law he has not told you," Aaliyah informed her mother. "Viviana's parents were killed in a suicide bombing while taking a holiday in Africa. We are not the only ones in this room who have lost much."

The older woman was quiet for a long moment. "Why did my son not tell me these things himself?"

"You were too busy being angered by his decision to marry her, ummi," Aaliyah said quietly.

An uncomfortable silence ensued. Viviana continued to shield her breasts as her mind drifted to memories of her mom and dad. She would give anything—literally anything—to hug them one last time. She supposed Muhammad's mother felt the same way about her sons, grandsons, and daughters-in-law. No matter what side of this war you were on, loss was loss and heartbreak was heartbreak.

"For whatever it's worth," Viviana admitted, "I am genuinely sorry for the loss of your children and grandchildren." She glanced away. "I am a translator, a linguist, not an interrogator." She shrugged with a dismissiveness she didn't feel. "When my people beat your son, I refused to translate for them until he was given medical attention, food, and water."

She didn't glance up to see whether that pronouncement was met with indifference, appreciation, or downright hatred. All she wanted was to go home—her real home—and have a good, long cry. Tears were something she would not shed in front of friends, much less enemies. Her one moment of weakness had already occurred when she'd unsuccessfully tried to escape. There would be no more moments of weakness, however fleeting.

Everything was finally getting to her. She couldn't remember ever being so completely overwhelmed. Considering the three most tragic events she'd experienced in life, namely the death of her parents, her near capture three years ago, and the siege that had successfully accomplished bringing her here now, that was saying a lot.

"Shukran." *Thank you.*

Viviana stilled. Her eyes widened in surprise as her gaze clashed with the older woman's. "Äafwan," she murmured. *You're welcome.*

Another, longer silence enveloped the palatial room. Finally Aaliyah delicately cleared her throat.

"I understand that you are not happy being here yet," Aaliyah said to Viviana. "Yet I hope one day that is not the case." She smiled a bit awkwardly. "My brother has asked my mother and me to prepare you for him so your body is not *haram* by our laws. I would be grateful if you made this easy on all of us."

Viviana inwardly sighed. She didn't want to acquiesce, yet the sweet girl made it difficult to deny her anything. Plus Viviana didn't know what kind of man Muhammad was. Would he beat his sister if she failed at the task he'd given her? She didn't know. For that reason and only that reason she gave a begrudging grunt of agreement.

"How badly is this 'sugaring' going to hurt?" Viviana asked.

"Sugaring?" the matriarch replied. Her eyebrows drew together. At last the beginnings of a smile tugged at her lips, though she resisted smiling fully. "We are not Muslim hillbillies," she informed Viviana. "Or Saudis."

"I must have not paid attention very well in class that day."

"We use wax, not sugar," Aaliyah said with a grin. "Much as your people do."

Waxing hurt like a motherfucker, but she supposed they already knew as much. It's not like she didn't upkeep her downstairs business anyway. The only hair Viviana had down there was a tiny triangular patch of dark gold.

She conceded again, though this time with an audible sigh. "Where should we do this? I imagine not on the bed."

\* \* \* \* \*

One thing Muhammad's mother would never be accused of was lacking in thoroughness. Jamila had waxed her three times from pussy hole to asshole, making certain not even a baby hair remained. When she'd finished she gave Viviana a peppermint and rosemary oil to rub all over her vulva so the pain would be non-existent by the time Muhammad came in to "consummate".

After the waxing, Aaliyah had removed the bandage from her arm. Noting that the bleeding had stopped, she'd wiped some sort of ointment on it and covered it with a clear Band-Aid.

By the time the two women got around to doing her makeup, Viviana didn't care about being naked anymore. She knew she'd care mightily when her captor walked in, but in front of the females she felt at ease.

"I think you will like this," Aaliyah told her as she finished contouring her eyebrows. "You were beautiful before, but *wallah*, you have the look of a fabled queen now."

Even Jamila grunted her agreement. Viviana decided the older woman would have made a formidable Russian dictator, but she said nothing.

"At least you will give me beautiful grandchildren," Jamila bluntly stated. One of her eyebrows darted up. "You do not take birth control do you?"

Oh how she wished she did. Unfortunately, Viviana had no reason to be on anything because she didn't have a partner. "No," she admitted.

Jamila inclined her head. "Good."

"*Wallah*," Aaliyah said, smiling, "I hope they have your eyes."

Viviana didn't know what to say to that so she said nothing. By the time the women took their leave, her nervousness had increased a thousand-fold. Sitting at the vanity next to a bathtub big enough to double as a swimming hole, she absently stared at herself in the mirror. Aaliyah could give any Hollywood makeup artist a run for their money. She didn't even feel as though she looked like herself and had told the younger woman so.

*"You look exactly like you," Aaliyah had returned. "All I did was exaggerate what is already there."*

Viviana sighed. This had been a wretchedly long day. She stood up and began the long walk toward the side of the vast room where the bed was. Any way she sliced it, there wasn't a way out of this night's upcoming event. Sure she could fight him off, but she was a realist. He was far too huge to deter for more than a few seconds.

Why did he want her? she wondered for the hundredth time. Marrying someone just to fuck them was a piss poor reason to ruin both their lives. Contrary to Aaliyah's professed hope, Viviana knew she'd never be happy here. Even if Muhammad grew on her by some unfathomable means, women served no purpose here other than to fuck and breed.

By the time she reached the bed and plopped down onto it, depression overruled her nervousness. She climbed under the blankets and laid her head down on one of the silk pillows.

Viviana sighed. She'd never been the type of starry eyed female to wistfully plan out her wedding day and wedding night years before so much as meeting the man she would eventually marry, but neither had she assumed it would be a hostage situation when and if it did happen.

# Chapter Five

Muhammad waited for as long as lust would allow. He wanted to give Viviana as much time as possible to accept her fate, even if he doubted such a capitulation would occur at any point in the foreseeable future. In her eyes they had known each other for a few days. For him it had been over two months—forever in his culture. Compounding that with the fact he had not been inside a woman since the death of his wives, his sexual need was great.

Wearing silky white serwal pajama pants and nothing else, Muhammad pushed a wheeled serving cart down the long corridor toward his suite. The trolley was loaded with a variety of foods and drinks he had taken the time to choose himself. His selections were based entirely on the provisions he knew Viviana most enjoyed from months of observing her and her eating habits. She would pretend to like falafel whenever one of her former housemates prepared it, but Chicken Sharwarma, hummus, and Fattoush salad made her eat with vigor and passion.

This was going to be a long night and would require much patience on his part. He didn't wish for her to fear him, yet he realized her apprehension was inevitable—at least for the present.

Already she had been his bride for four days, but because she had been asleep for three of them Muhammad had yet to give her the *mahr*—bride gift—that was required before consummating their marriage. That too was inside one of the many drawers of the serving trolley. While a part of him couldn't help but hope she liked his *mahr*, he was too pragmatic to expect anything beyond disdain from Viviana for quite some time.

His pulse picked up as he reached the doors to their apartment. He took a deep breath and slowly exhaled before opening them. He realized he had to keep his lust under control. At least for a little while longer.


Viviana heard the doors open, but she didn't acknowledge Muhammad's arrival. She continued to lie on her side, back facing him, and stare at nothing. The sound of squeaky wheels caused her curiosity to pique, but she didn't give in to the urge to turn on her right side and look at its source.

"I know from your breathing you are awake," Muhammad said.

She frowned, absently wondering how any human being could be *that* damn observant. The peculiar characteristic was simultaneously impressive and annoying.

"Correct," she admitted, seeing no reason to bother lying. "So let's just get this over with already."

"Your romantic nature is wooing me in ways I hadn't thought possible."

Was that amusement in his voice? She glowered, though he couldn't see it.

"What am I supposed to say?" Viviana asked drolly. "Oh goodie! It's time to be raped by a terrorist!"

He was silent for a protracted moment. She got a little nervous, wondering if she'd gone way too far way too soon.

"If my people invaded your country and forced our ways upon you, would you meekly submit or would you fight back?"

"I would fight back. But I wouldn't kill innocent civilians while doing it."

"Neither would I."

That pronouncement surprised her into silence. It was just as well for he wasn't done speaking. She continued to give him her back.

"I will not rape you," Muhammad said in a calm tone. There was a hint of irritation underscoring his words. "Though many of our women have suffered that fate at the hands of foreign invaders."

Viviana winced. She couldn't deny that ugly truth. Hell, she'd even been present when some allied soldiers had been arrested for that very crime and taken to God only knows where — presumably a military tribunal. Still...

"It happens both ways, you know. Your soldiers are pretty awful too."

"You were raped?" he quietly asked.

She sighed. Viviana hated thinking back on that awful night. "No. I was the only one al Qaeda didn't find. I hid under cleaning supplies in a janitorial closet."

He didn't speak for a long moment. "So that was you," Muhammad murmured. "The one that got away."

Viviana stilled. "You were there?"

"No. General Qabbani is a known enemy of mine. I was delighted by your escape."

Everything he said was in direct contrast to what trite intel she did know about him. He was confusing her, assuming anything he said could be believed. She pulled the covers tighter, still not facing him. "If you aren't going to rape me," she asked, steering the conversation back to the here and now, "then why did you have your mother—a real joy of a woman by the way!—prepare me for consummation?"

His tone was hesitant. "My mother was unkind with you?"

"Not at all. I love being called 'infidel' and 'kafir' while being blamed for every atrocity committed against your family. Did she attend *Hitler's Finishing School From Hell* by chance? Or was it Stalin's? *The Mussolini Academy for Making People Want To Choke You Out* maybe?" Viviana frowned, but begrudgingly gave him the truth. "Although she did become more tolerable as the day wore on."

She could hear Muhammad sigh. "I will speak with her. You should not be blamed for the deaths of my family any more than I should be blamed for the deaths of yours."

"Don't—please. I shouldn't have said anything. She'll only resent me more."

He grew silent. She could hear him sit down, presumably in one of the two chairs set on either side of the small, round table ten feet or so from the foot of the bed. The tension of the stark quiet frayed Viviana's nerves. She wished he'd speak yet hoped he didn't. The entire situation was confusing and overwhelming.

"Come sit at the table with me," Muhammad said with quiet resolve. "It is time for you to receive your *mahr*."

She blinked, for some reason stupefied he'd bothered buying her a bride-gift in the first place. Then again, sharia law required a *mahr* be given pre-consummation. Perhaps it wasn't surprising after all.

"Unless my *mahr* is clothing, I'm fine," Viviana muttered.

"You're behaving as a child again."

Her nostrils flared. "I am a captive—a hostage! And a naked one at that! What do you expect?"

Muhammad's typically calm demeanor cracked enough to let her hear some truthful emotion. She could hear him surge to his feet. "And you'd be as dead as your housemates had I not intervened!"

Viviana stilled. She sat up in bed and turned her head to face him. She kept the blanket covering her, shielding her nudity. "What are you talking—" Her eyes widened and her heartbeat picked up as her gaze landed on the half-naked and exceedingly chiseled face and body of Sheikh Muhammad al-Jihad al-Raqqah.

His closely cropped dark hair and sharp brown gaze gave way to a Roman nose and perfect lips. His towering frame was heavily muscled, his mocha-olive skin in sharp contrast to the white serwal pants he wore. Everything about him was massive — including the erection she could easily see delineated through his silky pants.

She swallowed a bit roughly. She had forgotten he was so handsome — as monsters go of course. Viviana doubted there was a pro-jihadi woman alive who wouldn't welcome the fate that had been forced on her. "What are you talking about?" she asked weakly.

The sheik sat back down. One of his dark eyebrows rose sardonically. Had he detected the twinge of innate arousal she'd experienced before masking it? The thought was depressing. Thankfully, he didn't humiliate her by bringing it up, much less taunt her with it, if he had noticed.

"Everyone in that 'safe' house was marked for death the moment you first entered its doors." His gaze seared into hers. "I was able to negotiate for one of your lives and only one. I," he said slowly, quietly, "chose you."

Viviana's pulse sped up. She blinked and looked away.

"It's war, Viviana. Do not tell me your people would not have done the same."

"I won't," she breathed out, staring into nothingness again, "because I can't."

Silence.

"I will not lie to you," Muhammad eventually said. "I chose you because I coveted you."

"So your cock decided which woman would live."

"Basically."

For some insane reason his words made her feel, if not better, at least less awful. Not because of the words themselves, but because of the unembellished truthfulness in them. Put plainly, she appreciated, even respected, his candor.

Viviana stood up, holding the blanket around her, and slowly walked to where Muhammad sat. Even seated the gigantic sheikh was nearly at eye level with her. His dark, unreadable gaze stayed trained on her every movement. She came to a halt directly in front of him.

"How long were the cameras there?" she asked.

"Before you arrived."

"How often did you watch me?"

"Every moment you weren't asleep. Sometimes even then."

She visibly stilled. "How often did you watch the others?"

"I didn't."

"Why?" she whispered.

"I coveted only you."

Viviana's pulse sped faster. A myriad of conflicting emotions, which ranged from anger to flattery, engulfed her. "I wasn't naked and masturbating most of the time."

"The word 'covet' isn't exclusive to lust, though sexual yearning was undeniably present."

"What else?"

He seemed uncomfortable discussing whatever *else* entailed, but she wanted to know the answer. "What else?" she asked again.

"I came to enjoy your sense of humor, your playfulness, your integrity and intellect." His gaze searched her face. "I fell in love with all the different pieces that comprise who you are."

Her round, turquoise eyes could only stare at him. This was a confession she hadn't been expecting.


The longer the ensuing silence grew, the more Muhammad wanted to kick himself for admitting to such frivolous emotions. He had enough of a challenge ahead of him where Viviana was concerned without his bride thinking him weak. He glanced away from her and absently ran a hand across his stubbly jaw.

"I will take my *mahr* now."

He stilled. His eyes widened. Determined not to betray further emotion, Muhammad steeled his voice to remain steady and controlled. "Your *mahr* comes in two parts," he said, opening one of the trolley's drawers, "though I only have the first with me." He picked up the piece of jewelry and shut it. "The part you receive before we consummate is, as I'm certain you're aware, required to be of monetary value. So I..."

His voice trailed off as his gaze returned to Viviana. She had dropped the blanket and stood before him completely naked. "I..." He swallowed heavily. "I chose this necklace for you."

*Wallah* she was more desirable than a thousand women combined. Lightly tanned skin, hair the color of dark gold, eyes a unique shade of the grass and sea combined, puffy lips, naturally big tits, thick rosy nipples...

He blew out a breath. And that said nothing of her curvy, womanly figure that was fleshy in all the right places. Or of her sexy, freshly waxed pussy that carried the scent of peppermint and rosemary.

"I bought this because it matches your eyes," Muhammad said thickly. He slowly stood up, not bothering to hide his painful erection. "And because I heard you say many times how beautiful you find these gems."

Viviana's gaze seemed to soften or perhaps it was wishful thinking on his part. Either way, she lifted her hair so he could clasp the jewelry around her neck. He took the strand of opals, emeralds, and diamonds and reverently did just that.

Without speaking a word, she turned around and walked toward their bed. His gaze grew heavy-lidded as he watched her plump ass jiggle with each step she took. Viviana climbed onto the bed, laid down on her back, and spread her legs wide open.

Muhammad's possessive, aroused gaze drank in the sight before him. He undid the drawstring of the serwal pants he wore and let them fall to the ground as he stared at her tight, pink pussy and huge tits with erect nipples. The *mahr* necklace she wore only added to her provocative appeal, the large emerald in the center resting between her breasts.

The bed sank a bit under his weight as he climbed onto it. He sat on his knees between her spread thighs and stared at all that belonged to him. He wanted to ask Viviana why she had relented, but feared she might change her mind if he broke the silence.

Muhammad slowly ran his battle-roughened hands all over her body. Starting at her navel, he worked his fingers upward, touching every silky inch of her skin. When he reached her breasts and his fingers began massaging her stiff nipples, both of their breathings hitched. She wouldn't make eye contact yet, which was just as well, for he wanted to play with the body he finally owned for as long as he pleased.

He spent the next ten minutes rubbing, massaging, and kissing all over her. By the time his lips latched onto one of her erect nipples and drew it into the heat of his mouth, Viviana was whimpering. He could tell his bride didn't want to be aroused, but her panting and soft moans gave away that she was.

Using his hands to hold her tits in place, Muhammad buried his face between them. He sucked on one nipple and then the other, his mouth hungrily going back and forth between them. He purred in the back of his throat as he shoved her tits together and swiped his tongue across both nipples in one long lick. She gasped, as aroused as he was, her hips instinctively raising up to welcome him inside.

Muhammad ignored her. His cock was so hard and his entire body so aroused he feared coming before he penetrated her, but he kept sucking on her sexy tits anyway. His heavy erection was pressed between them, wanting inside her cunt so badly that his balls ached. He ignored the pain and kept sucking her stiff nipples, wanting a verbal consent he knew Viviana didn't want to give him.

Her breathing grew heavier, her moans and gasps louder. She thrashed a bit beneath him, whimpering as she thrust her pussy up. He ignored her again, even if it was torturing him to do so. He purred around her nipples, sucking them harder.

"Please," she finally gasped.

He steeled himself, willing his need to orgasm away. Muhammad lifted his head, releasing her nipple with a pop. "Please what?" he murmured, his voice thick. He gazed into the sparkling eyes that refused to look at him. "Hmm? Please what?"

Her nostrils flared as her fiery gaze at last clashed with his. "Please fuck me," she ground out.

He pretended to mull her request over. His hesitation was all she could take.

"Please!" Viviana practically cried. The anger in her eyes turned to aroused desperation. "Whatever you want me to say," she panted out, "I'll say it."

Muhammad grabbed his cock by the root and pressed it against her tight, wet hole. She whimpered, wanting him inside. His jaw tightened. "Beg me by name," he told her in a gravelly tone. "Beg your husband to fuck you."

Viviana hesitated for a scant moment. Her breathing was heavy, her mouth apparently dry. She wet her lips before conceding. "Please, Muhammad," she panted.

She reared her hips up, trying to impale herself, but couldn't. He held firm.

*"Please Muhammad – my husband – please fuck me!"*

His large fingers ran through her hair before cradling her head. His jaw steeled and his nostrils flared. "Mine," he ground out.

Muhammad surged into her tight, sticky cunt, seating himself to the hilt. He groaned from the indescribable pleasure, the knowledge she now irrevocably belonged to him a powerful aphrodisiac.

He couldn't give her pussy time to adjust to his size. He had intended to start slow, but higher thinking eluded him. Muhammad fucked her cunt hard, his hips pistoning back and forth, his cock branding her as his with every stroke. She wrapped her legs around his waist, pulling him deeper inside her. Her moans of pleasure echoed in the bedroom.

*"Mine,"* he rumbled. *"All mine."*

He fucked Viviana like a primitive animal marking its territory. He growled as he plunged in and out of her tight cunt, fucking her harder and faster. The reverberations of flesh slapping against flesh resonated throughout the bedroom. The sound of hot, sticky pussy getting fucked and branded made his rigid cock impossibly stiffer.

"*Oh my God,*" Viviana gasped. "I'm—no!"

Her body needed to come, but her brain resisted. Muhammad craved her cum more than he wanted air to breathe. He fucked her like a man possessed, impaling her pussy over and over, again and again and again...

"*Oh my God!*"

Viviana's orgasm broke loose on a loud moan. Muhammad continued to pound her cunt hard, her gorgeous tits jiggling with every thrust. He groaned as her orgasm caused her pussy to contract, squeezing his large cock in a way he'd never before experienced.

"I'm coming, *habibti,*" he ground out. Every muscle in his body tensed. His jaw tightened. He plunged into her cunt harder and faster, deeper and more possessively. "I'm com— *Viviana!*"

Muhammad roared out the longest, hardest orgasm of his life. He kept fucking her mercilessly, pounding her pussy, hot cum spurting from his cock and filling her up with his cream. The primal animal inside him wanted her pregnant this very night so he didn't slow his gait until her cunt had milked him for every drop of seed he had to give.

He looked down into her face, his gaze piercing hers, as his strokes slowed and ebbed. Sweat soaked both their bodies. Their breathing, gradually returning to normal, was still labored.

"You are no longer my bride, but my wife," Muhammad panted out. Forming complete sentences was too taxing so he focused on the important part. "You are mine. Only mine."

He held her gaze for what felt an eternity. After a long moment, she inclined her head, acknowledging his claim.

Arrogantly satisfied, Muhammad collapsed beside her. He forced her to lie on top of him, holding her closely as they drifted off into sleep.

# Chapter Six

Viviana awoke in the middle of the night feeling dazed and confused. Muhammad was still asleep so she quietly lifted her body from his and got off the bed. Walking toward the bathing basin, her emotions tormented, she couldn't help but feel as though she'd capitulated with little resistance. Actually, zero resistance. She had *begged him* to fuck her.

He had called her *habibti* in the heat of sex, she recalled, walking into the water. It was like calling a woman "baby" or "darling" in English, but she suspected the word carried more sentiment for Muhammad because he didn't seem the type to toss it around lightly. In that way, *habibti* was probably closer in meaning to "beloved" for him.

Her teeth sank into her lower lip as she used a clean cloth to wash herself. Viviana felt engulfed in a chaotic haze, troubled by what she was supposed to think or feel.

Muhammad had saved her life. He had done it for sex, or at least that was his initial motivation according to his own narrative, but he *had* spared her. She stilled, recalling something odd he'd said earlier.

*"Everyone in that 'safe' house was marked for death the moment you first entered its doors. I was able to negotiate for one of your lives and only one. I chose you."*

Why would Muhammad al-Jihad al-Raqqah, second only to the self-proclaimed caliph of the Daesh, need to negotiate with anyone? The only logical explanation was al-Baghdadi, terrorist number one, had plotted the deaths of her colleagues himself.

So how did Muhammad factor into all of this? And how on earth had he escaped? Viviana threw the cloth to the tiled floor beside the basin as another memory struck.

*"You managed to get a qadi to act as the wali of an American hostage?" Viviana released the blanket and threw her hands in the air. Fuck being naked. She no longer cared. "Wait until my government finds out about this bullshit!"*

*Muhammad was silent for a long moment. His gaze lingered at her naked breasts before returning to her face. "Do you honestly believe they don't already know?" he murmured.*

Muhammad hadn't escaped. He'd been freed by the highest echelons of her own nation.

But why?


"What are you thinking?"

Viviana's head shot up. She hadn't heard him get out of bed. It was still the middle of the night. For whatever reason she'd assumed he would sleep until dawn.

Wrapped in a large bathing towel and seated at one of the two chairs at the table near the bed, she cleared her throat. "Lots of things."

His eyebrows rose. "I see you are bathed. I will do the same and join you for the meal we should have eaten earlier."

"I'm not hungry."

"Get hungry. You need food."

Viviana sighed, but didn't argue. She was wise enough to choose her battles. Arguing over an issue she knew he was right about didn't exactly qualify as prudent.

Ten minutes later, still lost in thought, she was jilted into the here and now when Muhammad took his seat at the table across from her. A bathing towel shielded his lower half, but his chiseled arms and chest were still bared. She blew out a breath. It would have been easier to resist his desire to consummate if he didn't look like *that*. Then again, how handsome and masculine he was or wasn't wouldn't have factored into the equation for her at all had he not treated her with such warmth and worry.

He was driving her insane. That had to be it.

"Tell me your thoughts," Muhammad said as he opened the drawers to the serving cart.

She saw no reason not to be blunt. The man had a way of knowing when she wasn't being candid with him anyway. "I am confused," Viviana began. She wet her lips as he pulled Chicken Sharwarma, hummus, and Fattoush salad out of the cart and placed them on the table. Her eyes widened even as her belly started to rumble. "How did...?" She rubbed her temples. "You really paid attention to everything, didn't you?"

He didn't smile, but she could see a sparkle in his brown eyes. "Everything concerning you, yes."

There he went again, saying stuff that made her feel like he cared. It was a feeling she hadn't known since her mom and dad were killed. Maybe he knew that too and was using it to get under her skin.

Plates of plump dates, figs, and traditional Syrian sweets were placed on top of the serving cart, which Muhammad then pulled closer to the table. Viviana's mouth watered. If she hadn't been hungry before, she was famished now.

"The Fattoush salad I made myself. Your colleague did not prepare it for you properly so I hope you enjoy the way it's supposed to taste." He reached across the table and placed a bowl of it in front of her. "Your fork is beside you."

Viviana immediately went for the utensil and dug in. She didn't want to cater to his vanity, but she couldn't stop her eyes from rolling back into her head. "Oh my God," she said after swallowing the first bite, "this is incredible."

He grinned. It was the first time she'd noticed that the hardened warlord had dimples. They made him seem…human. Uncomfortable, she lowered her gaze and kept eating.

"So tell me your thoughts," Muhammad again instructed her. He picked up his fork and started eating a bowl of Fattoush salad as well. "Come now."

Viviana swallowed another bite. "Can we eat first? I was taught never to speak with food in my mouth and there is going to be food in my mouth for at least ten more minutes."

"Of course." There was that sparkle in his dark gaze again. "I'm glad you like it."

She hesitated. Viviana didn't know how a woman in her position was supposed to react, but there was something that needed said regardless to everything else. "Thank you."

Muhammad swallowed the bite in his mouth and shrugged. "Waiting to talk until you've eaten is a simple request. I'll always oblige you when I can."

"I meant for the food."

He stilled. His gaze found hers. The food went deeper than the request to put off talking and they both knew it. He had gone to great lengths to ensure she would have a meal on her wedding night—forced or not—that she would enjoy.

"You're welcome," he murmured.

They ate and drank in comfortable silence for what turned out to be another twenty minutes. Everything tasted so good, all the dishes' ingredients so fresh. When Viviana plopped a sweet, sticky date into her mouth she was certain this feast was as close to manna from heaven as it got. The dates back home were good, but they didn't taste like candy.

At the end of the meal, Muhammad poured them both a glass of wine. Her jaw dropped a bit. Observant Muslims never imbibe alcohol and that was a Parisian label. France wasn't exactly known for producing *halal*—permitted—wine by skipping the fermentation part.

"The prophet—peace be upon him—enjoyed fermented wine," Muhammad told her, obviously reading her expression. "Nowhere in the Qur'an are believers forbidden from drinking wine. They are forbidden only from excess and drunkenness. Imams made up the rest."

Viviana realized she wore the expression of a shocked simpleton. "I know that, but I've never heard a Muslim admit that out loud."

A small smile tugged at his lips. "There is a difference between serving Allah in reverence and making up rules to suit the whims of men."

"The Qur'an doesn't state women are to be veiled either."

"I do not argue this point with you. Again, the veil falls under the heading of 'whims of men'."

She blinked. Viviana was a learned woman. She'd heard a few feminist Muslim women—all branded as heretics—make the same argument, but she hadn't expected to hear it come from the mouth of a traditionalist, much less a male one. She took a sip from the wine as she studied him. "Christians do that too, you know."

"Do what?"

She took another drink before answering. "Disregard the reality of our sacred book and allow men who think they know more than everyone else to interpret the passages for us." She set down her glass. "Their interpretations are usually wrong."

"You are that confident in your knowledge?" he mused.

"I'm a logical thinker, not an emotional one." She shrugged. "Nor am I easily led."

His expression was unreadable. "I believe you."

"Well that and I also speak, read, and write all the archaic languages the books were originally inscribed in." Viviana cleared her throat before changing the subject. "You wanted to know what I was thinking about..."

Muhammad inclined his head. "I still do."

"I don't even know where to begin." She audibly exhaled. "I've got a lot of questions."

His eyes raked over her cleavage—and the *mahr* dangling between them—before returning to her face. "Then start asking them."

She looked away. "I'm not so sure I want to hear the answers," she muttered.

He said nothing, only stared at her. Viviana realized he was being patient and giving her the time she needed to collect her thoughts. What she couldn't understand yet again was *why*. Muhammad al-Jihad al-Raqqah held all the cards here. She nibbled at her lower lip. The man was an enigma.

"Okay," she finally said, breaking the silence, "let's start with what I hope are easy questions."

"Go on."

She held up a hand and started ticking off questions with her fingers. "Number one: will I ever be given clothes to wear? Number two: will I ever be allowed out of this room? Number three: will I ever be permitted to go home? Number four—"

"Yes, yes, and no," Muhammad interrupted. He frowned, apparently irritated by the third question. His next words confirmed her supposition. "I do not think *my wife* understands what it means to be married."

Viviana matched him frown for frown. "No. No, I don't." She splayed her hands. "A very astute observation on your part."

His jaw tightened. "Do not," he bit out, every word overly enunciated, "speak to me with disrespect in your voice."

Her nostrils flared. "I didn't, but why not?"

"Because I do not speak that way to you."

No he didn't, yet neither did she. Apparently he believed otherwise. "I'm sorry," she muttered, trying to keep the peace.

"Your tone isn't convincingly apologetic, but I'll accept it. This time."

He should feel grateful she apologized at all. She was a hostage for fuck's sake! "I don't have any more questions," Viviana announced, sighing. She stood up, avoiding eye contact. "Thank you for answering the ones I asked," she said as steadily as possible. She walked toward her side of the bed, turning to face him once there. Forcing a meek tone and casting her gaze to the ground she asked, "Do I have your permission to sleep?"

A long, unnerving silence ensued. She might have been looking at the tiled floor, but she could feel Muhammad's gaze blazing into her. It felt like forever and then some had passed by before he spoke.

"*Yalla!*" Muhammad barked. *Come here!*

Viviana's head jarred up. Her turquoise eyes widened in surprise and nervousness. Now what had she done? She swallowed a bit roughly before obeying his command. She walked to where he sat and stood before him, careful to keep her gaze lowered. She didn't have it in her to argue with him right now so she was doing her best to behave in accordance with Sharia law.

She was never going home. That had been a difficult answer to hear. All she wanted to do was get under the covers and cry undetected.

"Look me in the eye," Muhammad instructed.

Viviana immediately obeyed. His expression was stoic, unreadable. Her apprehension grew.

"Why," he asked with forced patience, "are you behaving this way?"

Her round eyes grew rounder. "What do you mean?"

Muhammad's jaw tightened. He started cursing in a dialect of Arabic even she didn't know.

"What have I done *now?!*" Viviana all but whined. Holy shit! She was this close to losing the fragile rein she had on her emotions. "I am trying to behave respectfully!"

"You are trying to anger me!"

"By being compliant?"

"Yes!"

"There's no winning with you!" She threw her hands up. "If I say what I'm thinking you get mad and if I keep it to myself you get mad! I give the fuck up!"

"I want you to be you! Not some caricature of a Muslim wife!"

Viviana's eyes narrowed in dawning comprehension. "I *seeeeee*," she drew out.

He grunted. "What do you see?"

"You want me to be me, but only the parts of me you like." Her face flushed with irritation. "Well life doesn't work like that. If you truly want *me* then you take all of who I am. Otherwise," she gritted out, "you get the caricature."

Muhammad looked away, but said nothing. She could see he knew she was right even if he wasn't ready to admit it.

"I just found out I will never see my home again," Viviana said. "The house filled with memories of my parents, the garden I've tended in my backyard since I was old enough to help my mom, the chair my dad rocked me to sleep in as a child…" Tears stung the backs of her eyes, but she refused to let them fall. "I want to climb into that bed and cry for what I've lost if it's okay with you."

His gaze found hers. His expression was still unreadable, but the muscles in his face had relaxed. "Yes, of course," he murmured.

She inclined her head. Turning on her heel, she slowly walked back to the bed.

"Viviana," Muhammad called out just as she was climbing under the covers. She paused to look at him.

"Two more things," he said.

Her eyebrows rose. "Yes?"

"I wish for you to sleep naked beside me," Muhammad instructed.

"Okay." His brooding gaze watched her remove the towel and toss it to the floor. "And the second thing?" she inquired.

"I want all of who you are."

Viviana stilled. Something in the vicinity of her heart wrenched. There he went again, making her feel like he cared. "Thank you," she said quietly.

* * * * *

Still seated at the table, Muhammad watched his wife's body repeatedly spasm from under the covers. Viviana made no sound, but even had she not told him she needed to cry he would have recognized that she was. Thirty-five minutes had passed since his wife climbed into their bed—thirty of them had been spent like this. It was fucking heartbreaking.

He was a man renowned for overlooking nothing, yet he'd neglected to anticipate how Viviana would feel about never seeing her home again. He'd known about the death of her parents—that news was in every intelligence report he'd obtained. What he had not realized was she'd continued to dwell in her childhood home all these years later. He sighed. In her eyes, she must feel as though she'd lost her parents twice.

Muhammad's reaction to the death of his family had fueled an opposite reaction in him. He'd ordered what was left of his former estate burned to the ground so he'd never again have to see the walls that reminded him of his sons. He wasn't certain if he or Viviana was the foolish one. Perhaps both of them were too extreme in their choices—her for still clinging to the past, him for attempting to forget it.

* * * * *

Viviana awoke on a moan, disoriented and aroused. She breathed heavily as her sleep-addled brain tried to assemble a coherent picture out of what was happening to her. She knew she had come—she just didn't know why. The pleasure was so intense and all-consuming…

"I do not like for you to cry," Muhammad murmured against her ear. His breathing was as raspy as hers. "It breaks my heart for you."

She stilled, the nonsensical at last making sense. Muhammad had made her come—and he was buried deep inside her.

Viviana didn't resist his long, languid strokes, but instead wrapped her arms around his neck and rocked her hips up to meet his thrusts. Even if things could never be idyllic for them outside of bed, at least they possessed the requisite mutual attraction for passion inside of it. Sex wasn't everything, but it was something, and she'd never needed to be wanted more than she did right now.

She had fallen asleep with indescribably painful emotions engulfing her. That turmoil had followed into her dreams, forcing them to twist into nightmares. Mental images of loneliness, desolation, war, and chaos. A demon laughing. Her boss trading her for intel without so much as blinking...

Muhammad picked up the pace, impaling her with his cock in fast, hard strokes. She gasped, the pleasure erasing the haunting images. "I wish things could always be like this between us," Viviana admitted without thinking. Her head lulled back.

"They can," Muhammad told her, his voice gravelly. He kissed the throat she'd bared to him. "And eventually they will."

She didn't think she was capable of completely accepting life on Syrian terms, but she said nothing. Before the Daesh had come into power, Syria had been a lovely country with freedoms it might never again have. Now it was desolate and war-torn, Shi'a Muslims escaping the land as desperately as Christians. Last she'd heard, even most Sunnis were fleeing.

Viviana cast off all thoughts not a part of the here and now. She moaned as Muhammad plunged in and out of her, his animalistic fucking as possessive as it was primal. Her hands fell from around his neck and found his back. He growled as her fingernails instinctively dug into him, scratching his flesh as she groaned out another orgasm.

He fucked her harder, her pussy making suctioning sounds on every outstroke. She gasped as he impaled her cunt, his breathing and muscular tension telling her he was close to coming.

"*Hayda kesse,*" Muhammad ground out. *This is my pussy.*

She groaned, her tits jiggling with every thrust. Her teeth sank into his neck, driving him over the edge.

His fucking became maniacal, branding. "A'am yeje ma'e," he rasped. *I'm coming.*

Muhammad came on a roar, plunging in and out of her pussy as hot cum spurted from his cock and warmed her insides. Her cunt contracted, milking him for every drop he had to give.

This time when he collapsed next to her and nudged her to sleep on his chest, Viviana immediately complied. Insane as it might have been, she needed to be close to him right now.

Tomorrow was soon enough to deal with how she felt about the constant chinks he assaulted her armor with.

# Chapter Seven

The next couple of months passed by with little clothing and the ability to leave the bedroom only while in Muhammad's escort. If she was in their suite, he wanted her naked. Outside of the room, she was clothed, but had to remain within his sight. Most of her time was spent sequestered in the boudoir with nary a stitch of clothing. While the chamber was closer in size to a small house than a bedroom, it was still confining. She hated it.

The hour or so every few days that she was given clothing and the ability to leave the bedroom was mostly spent with Aaliyah. She was growing very fond of Muhammad's little sister who always took the time to buy Viviana books to read and play board games with her. Jamila was never around, which was a good thing. The al-Raqqah matriarch was more than she felt up to dealing with.

Every time Viviana and Aaliyah played a game together, they would end up laughing and sharing stories. Muhammad would sit on the far side of the library, a brooding expression on his face. As soon as the game came to an end, he would invariably stand up and escort Viviana back to what she mentally referred to as her posh prison cell. The second the doors to the bedroom were closed, he ripped off whatever she was wearing and fucked her hard, like he didn't want her to forget he owned her.

Muhammad fucked her three times a day—at minimum. His sex drive was undeniably high, but she sensed he had difficulty accepting emotion outside of bed and had come to associate being inside Viviana as being loved by Viviana. She couldn't deny he was growing on her. Even imprisoned as she was, she'd never felt more needed by anyone—ever.

On the downside, she was starting to feel like one of those life-size "Real Dolls". Her only purpose in life in so far as she could tell was to be a naked and waiting cum receptacle. One evening over dinner, nude as always, she became disgruntled enough to finally tell him exactly that.

"You are my wife, not a doll!"

"Yeah? So this is a marriage to you? Being locked up in this room sixty-nine hours of every seventy-two just isn't cutting it for me."

"I have my reasons," Muhammad said cryptically. "They aren't as selfish as you think."

"Keeping me naked isn't selfish?"

"That part is, but not the rest."

Viviana frowned. "Then why?"

"I cannot say yet."

"When can you say?"

"I do not yet know."

She huffed, but said nothing else. Stabbing the meat on her plate with a fork, she jabbed a piece of it into her mouth.

"Why must you wear clothes when it is only the two of us in here?" Muhammad asked.

"I mustn't do anything," she muttered. "The point is having a choice. *You* aren't naked. You're still in formal attire minus your head-scarf."

"It is bad that I enjoy seeing my wife in a way no other man ever will?"

"You're purposely turning this around on me. I'm not an idiot."

He grunted. "I prefer you naked."

Viviana dropped the fork and splayed her hands. "Your preference is my command. Now if only you could figure out a way to deflate the air out of me when you're finished playing with your toy then you wouldn't have to hear me bitch."

"You have lowered yourself in status from a 'Real Doll' to the blow-up kind," Muhammad murmured. There was no mistaking his thinly veiled amusement. "Too much work for me when I prefer to play with my toy as much as possible."

She narrowed her eyes at him. He sighed.

"Viviana, the less people who know you are here, the better. For now." Muhammad's expression grew serious. "I will explain everything at the proper time. Just know this sentence of what I'm sure you feel is imprisonment will be over soon."

She blinked. Her stomach lurched. Had he changed his mind? Was he letting her go?

She wished that scenario held the same allure it once did. Viviana blew out a breath as the truth struck her hard—Sheikh Muhammad al-Jihad al-Raqqah had gotten under her skin. She should be doing the happy dance at the mere possibility of freedom, but she felt instead like a child whose balloon was just popped.

Viviana told herself she no longer cared. Her nostrils flared as she stood up and pushed away from the table. Preparing to make her way to the bed and crawl under the covers, she was stopped when Muhammad's hand seized her wrist.

"What is wrong with you now?" he barked.

"You! And let go of me!"

"Now what have I done?!"

She swiped away a rogue tear with her free hand. He noticed, of course, his expression growing more concerned.

"Viviana." He stood up and placed his hands on her shoulders. "If you are that upset about being naked in our bedroom I will bring you clothes."

"It's not that," she admitted in a dejected voice.

"Then what, *hayati*?" he asked gently.

*Hayati.* The literal translation was *my soul*. It was a term of affection that carried more weight, intimacy, and love than *habibti* could ever aspire to. Viviana felt like a caged animal that needed a good roar.

"You can't just...!" Her face scrunched up in anger, insult, and hurt. "You can't just steal someone, force them to marry you, make them care about you, and then say, 'Guess what? You'll be free to leave soon.' That was a shitty thing to do! I would rather you had beaten me the entire time so I'd be a hundred percent happy about being paroled!"

His jaw dropped. "You care for me?"

She rolled her eyes. "Of course I care, you ass!"

If she could have smacked the smile off his face, she would have. Unfortunately, his hands were still pinning her shoulders. "Good," he murmured, "Because if I thought I was in love with you before you came here, I have definitely fallen in love with you since your arrival."

Viviana opened her mouth to yell at him, but was forestalled by his confession. She blinked a few times, confused. "But you said I was getting out of prison soon," she said dumbly.

His frown was severe. "I meant this room, not my life!" He let go of one of her shoulders so he could slash his hand through the air. He loved doing that to underscore a point. "You will never be released from this marriage whether you feel imprisoned or not!"

"Good!"

"Good?"

"You're driving me insane, but yeah! Good!"

His eyes flared. "It's the other way around," he ground out.

Muhammad whirled her around and bent her over the bed. She could hear him remove his clothes as forcefully as he usually removed hers. "I cannot believe you thought for a second I'd let you leave me," he growled. He spanked her hard on the ass, causing her to yelp. "You are mine!"

They both groaned as he impaled Viviana from behind, his long, thick cock buried to her core. He fucked her hard,

97

pummeling in and out of her cunt in merciless, possessive plunges. "My pussy," he rasped, fucking her faster, "Only mine."

Viviana met his thrusts with her own, throwing her hips back to meet his every stroke. The sound of her pussy getting fucked, of tight, wet flesh being rapidly penetrated by hard muscle, was one she knew he found as arousing as she did. Muhammad groaned as he fucked her harder, burying himself inside her over and over, again and again. Viviana's tits jiggled with every thrust, her body's positioning causing her nipples to be more sensitive than usual.

"I'm coming," she gasped, the pleasure his cock brought her so intense. "I'm coming."

"Give me your cum," he gritted out, fucking her hard. He spanked her ass again. "Give me *my* cum."

The knot of sexual tension in her belly uncoiled, erupting so hard she could feel her womb contract. She moaned like a wounded animal as she came the hardest she'd ever come in her life.

Muhammad fucked her even faster, his stiff cock impaling her over and over, again and again. She could hear his breath suck in and feel his muscles tense.

"I'm coming *hayati*," he rasped. "I—*oh fuck!*"

He came on a roar, his cock spurting hot cum deep inside her. He continued to fuck her cunt while he emptied himself, mumbling like a madman about her and her pussy belonging to him forever.

When it was over, they both crawled up onto the bed and collapsed. She fell asleep curled up in his embrace, feeling safe and secure…

And needed.

# Chapter Eight

A few mornings later, Viviana awoke to a half empty bed. Muhammad was nowhere to be seen. It was probably good she finally had some time to herself because she needed to sort out her tumultuous emotions.

He'd admitted last night that he wanted her to refer to him as her husband when she spoke to others about him. When Viviana pointed out Aaliyah was the only person besides him she could speak to, Muhammad had been unmoved. "Then refer to me as your husband in front of my sister," he'd grumbled.

For whatever reason, calling him "my husband" to others signified one hundred percent capitulation in his mind. Truthfully, she could understand why. He was quick to refer to Viviana as his wife even if she was the only person in the room, but Viviana never referred to him as her husband.

She sighed. She supposed it signified one hundred percent capitulation to her as well.

While her heart felt married, her stubborn mind still insisted she was a hostage and that any self-respecting hostage wouldn't yield. She could have great sex with Muhammad and was now permitted to care about him, but that's where her mind drew its line in the sand. The word *love* was a no-no to her obstinate brain so it was little wonder committing to being married for life to the sheikh was meeting with major resistance from her head.

She blinked away the conflicting feelings, no longer wanting to deal with them. Glancing around, she realized she must have slept quite soundly because even the dishes they'd left on the table last night had been cleaned up. She squinted as she looked at the bare slab, noticing a single piece of paper set on it. Curious, she got out of bed to read the note scrawled in Arabic:

*My Dearest Viviana,*

*After you bathe, check the closet nearest the water for clothing. My sister Aaliyah took the time to pick the items out for you so please pretend to admire them even if you do not. (We can always buy you new clothes later.)*

*The doors to our apartments are unlocked. Once dressed, follow the hallway to the doors you attempted to escape through your first conscious night here – not the ones we walk through when going to the library. I await you there, as does your breakfast.*

*Your Husband,*

*Muhammad*

Viviana couldn't help but grunt out a begrudging smile courtesy of His Bluntness. No other man would consider reminding her of her thwarted attempt at a getaway except for Muhammad. To him it was merely the simplest, quickest method of explaining where he was.

Ten minutes later and freshly bathed, Viviana leafed through the assortment of kaftans Aaliyah had procured her. The vibrant colors and jeweled fabrics were top shelf so she wouldn't have to pretend at all. Since there were no hijabs, niqabs, or burkas to be found, she assumed it was okay not to wear a head covering. If Muhammad was the only man currently in residence, that made sense.

In the end, Viviana chose a silk turquoise dress with gold and gemstones embroidered around the neck and at the sides. A pair of gold high heels accented the aqua-green kaftan quite regally. Uncomfortable with how shapeless the dress hung, she pulled a gold scarf too sheer to be a hijab from the closet and fashioned a belt out of it. That accomplished, she spent the next ten minutes doing her makeup and hair. She was liberal with the black kohl, mascara, and red lipstick fashionable for Syrian women, but didn't bother with the layers of foundation, concealer, and rouge that screamed *drag queen* to her. Her hair she left cascading down into dark gold curls.

Dressed and more than a little hungry, Viviana did as the note instructed and made her way down the long corridor until she reached the set of doors. As promised, they opened. On the other side was a decadently gilded atrium that appeared to be the epicenter of the estate. Various hallways branched off from it, like the legs of a posh, golden spider. Unsure where she was supposed to go, she followed the sound of voices down the hallway directly across from where she stood.

"There she is!" Aaliyah enthused, standing up. Viviana smiled at her as she entered the rotund dining room. "I knew you would choose that dress! Didn't I say she would, Momo?"

Muhammad's dark gaze was unreadable as usual, yet something told Viviana he was pleased with her look. "Naam." *Yes.* "You did, Aaliyah."

"Why the belt?" Jamila asked in her typical condescending tone.

Viviana pasted a fake smile on her face. She hadn't seen Muhammad's mother since the waxing and would have chosen to keep the status quo intact had it been up to her. It didn't matter. She would not let that woman ruin her first day as a parolee. "Because I prefer the dress to have some shape rather than hang from my body like a burlap sack."

Jamila harrumphed. "I'm given to understand your marriage to my son has been well consummated so I will overlook your desire to dress wantonly. Today."

"Ummi," Muhammad bit out.

Viviana held up a palm. "No, it's okay. Now tell me how you really feel, Jamila."

Aaliyah's gaze flew to the tabletop. Muhammad sighed as he ran a hand over his jawline.

"If you must know," Jamila stated, "I do not feel you are good enough for my son."

The question had been rhetorical, but fuck it. Apparently she wanted to go there.

"Ummi!" Muhammad bellowed. "Enough!"

"She asked," Jamila replied defensively. "I answered."

Viviana sat down next to her monster-in-law just to irritate her. She kept the fake smile plastered on her lips. "Were your sons last two wives good enough for him?"

"Of course," Jamila huffed. "They were God-fearing women."

"Ummi," Aaliyah said in the naïve way she had about her, "you didn't like them either."

Muhammad resumed rubbing his jaw. Jamila's face colored. Viviana went in for the kill.

"It sounds to me, Jamila, that you're accustomed to wielding all the power around here and dislike anyone you think might usurp you." She splayed her hands. "Well guess what? If your idea of 'God-fearing' is 'Jamila-fearing' you're in for a hell of a bad ride."

The matriarch's nostrils flared. "Muhammad. You will not permit your *kafir* wife to speak to me like this." When her son said nothing, her face flushed with anger. "Muhammad!"

"He hasn't gone deaf," Viviana announced as she heaped food onto her plate. "But I can promise you this," she continued, not bothering to look at the atrocious woman seated next to her, "This is *my* home now too. I won't tolerate being belittled in it."

Jamila gasped. Aaliyah and Muhammad wore surprised expressions.

"I am more than willing to not interfere with how you prefer to do things," Viviana said, still piling food onto her plate, "so long as you are willing to play nice."

"I do not need your permission to—"

"Oh, but you do," Viviana interjected. Finished serving herself, she turned her attention to Jamila. "Your son and I have decided to make our marriage work out." She realized this was news to Muhammad—a quick glance in his direction confirmed that—but then it was news to Viviana as well. "So when it comes right down to it, do you really want to force your own son to choose between us?"

Jamila's nostrils flared. "It's a contest you will lose."

Viviana's fake smile grew wider. "Your harping versus my body in his bed. I somehow doubt it."

Jamila gasped. "You have no class!"

"I have plenty of class when the person I'm speaking to earns it," Viviana returned. Her turquoise eyes flashed. "I will not be kowtowed by you like Muhammad's last two wives were." She picked up her fork. "'Begin as you mean to go on' my mom always said. And so I do." When Jamila opened her mouth to speak, Viviana forestalled whatever she was about to say. "If you speak one ill word against my dead mother, I will never forgive you for it. Never."

Jamila's face colored, but she wisely held her tongue. Furious, she stood up, shoved away from the dining table, and briskly walked off to wherever in the hell it was escaped Nazis go.

Viviana slammed her fork into the pile of food on her plate. She grunted as she shoved a heaping bite of eggs into her mouth.

Dr. Lincoln was pissed off and she didn't care if Muhammad was angry about the confrontation or not. There was only so much disrespect a person could take and Jamila had exceeded her limit long ago.

"That was wonderful," Aaliyah whispered.

Viviana's eyes rounded. Her head came up as she swallowed the bite of eggs. "I thought you'd be upset that I spoke to your mother in such a way."

"Not when she makes a habit of behaving as she does," Aaliyah corrected. "She has scared off every potential husband I've ever held an interest in. I feel as though she wishes for me to be stuck with her for life." She nudged her brother. "I've been telling Momo for years that enough is enough already."

Muhammad frowned. "In Islam, we do not cast the widows, especially our own mothers, aside like trash." He sighed. "Viviana, please at least try to get along with her."

Viviana resumed eating without comment. She behaved as if she hadn't heard him.

"Viviana," Muhammad ground out. "Do not ignore me."

"I-I should go," Aaliyah said uncomfortably. She made to stand. "I hope to spend time with you later, sister. I—"

"There's no need to leave," Viviana said with forced cheer. "If he's choosing good old ummi over me you might as well be present to hear it."

A tic began to work in his jaw. "I never said that. I am merely disappointed at your rude behav—"

Viviana stood up and shoved away from the table in much the way Jamila-the-Hun had. "She questioned my clothing, said I dress like a whore, and stated I wasn't good enough for you all before I even sat down," Viviana said through gritted teeth. "She then called me *kafir* again, which by the way you didn't take her to task for, and *I* am the one whose behavior disappoints you?" Her eyes narrowed. "I'm quite disappointed in the behavior of my self-proclaimed husband too."

"Viviana!"

She ignored him and marched back toward her prison cell. So much for working out her marriage to Sheikh Shithead. "I suggest you nail up all the doors to this fucking estate," she threw out over her shoulder, "because I'm running at the first opportunity."

Muhammad frowned at his sister who was already frowning at him. "What?" he snapped.

"I couldn't stand your first two wives any more than could ummi, probably because they were just like her with their guilt, control, and manipulations. I cherished my nephews, but Nouf and Amal?" Aaliyah shook her head. "Not a bit."

"You know as well as I do that those were political marriages. It is beneath you to speak ill of the dead, Liyah."

"You miss my point, Momo."

"Then what is it?"

"Finally you marry a woman who doesn't have a manipulative, deceitful bone in her body and you dare to pretend the trouble between her and ummi is Viviana's?" Aaliyah clucked her tongue. "The woman even warned you she plans to run! Who is that honest?"

He didn't know whether to laugh or groan so the sound that came out of him was a mixture of both. "Yes she did, didn't she?"

Aaliyah smiled. "I don't know what happened to ummi after daddy died, but she's out of control and we both know it. Momo, every day she becomes more intolerable! I know she is our mother, but you are the head of this household. The responsibility of her behavior lies with you in the eyes of Allah."

Muhammad was well aware of that fact. He didn't know how to handle the delicate situation so he hadn't yet broached it. It was apparent he now had to. It was either that or purchase approximately one hundred thousand nails. "I will deal with this as soon as we reach Raqqah."

Aaliyah's eyebrows rose. "We're returning to the United Arab Emirates?"

"It isn't safe here. Not so long as al-Baghdadi remains in power."

"I thought—"

He raised his hand. "Say nothing until we're safely gone."

Aaliyah slowly nodded. "When do we leave?"

"The plane is being fueled as we speak."

She blew out a breath. "*Wallah,* I am so pleased with this decision. I'm going mad here with nothing to do!"

Muhammad stood up. He bent his head and kissed his sister atop hers. "You are wrong about one thing, Liyah."

"What is that?"

"I will not let ummi keep you with her forever. I will begin searching for a suitable husband when we're out of this Godforsaken land."

Aaliyah grinned. "When I was a child you promised me I would have the final say."

"I neither forget nor break my promises." He sighed. "Now if you'll excuse me I have a wife to carry kicking and screaming to the plane."

\* \* \* \* \*

Unfortunately, Muhammad's prediction wasn't far off. Viviana didn't bother with screaming, but she did a hell of a lot of kicking and protesting. She dropped her full body weight to the ground, which amounted to nothing for Muhammad. Throwing her over his shoulder like a sack of potatoes, she burned his ears with every expletive under the sun and some new ones he'd never heard. He bemusedly decided his favorite was "Sheikh Shithead". When he announced that meant she was "Sheikha Shithead" she became impossibly more furious, pounding on his back with her fists to underscore as much.

Finally, all four of them were on his private plane and well out of Syrian airspace. Only two of the passengers were speaking to each other—Muhammad and Aaliyah. His mother and his wife both sat in their seats, arms crossed over their chests, both of them feigning an interest in the clouds outside their windows. Viviana might not have been like ummi in many ways, but when it came to pouting they were more or less twins.

"I'm sorry."

Muhammad's head shot up at the sound of his mother's voice. She continued to stare out the window, but the words had been spoken. He just wasn't certain to whom.

"Me too."

This from Viviana. She too didn't look away from the window. Muhammad's eyebrows rose.

"I have become a bitter old woman," his mother said. "I don't blame you for hating me."

"I don't hate you," Viviana muttered. "The only hate I have in my heart is reserved for whoever killed my parents."

Muhammad and Aaliyah stole a bewildered glance at each other. They both decided to stay quiet.

"Can we start over?" Jamila asked.

"I'm agreeable to that," Viviana replied.

"I am sorry my son—Sheikh Shithead—stole your freedom."

Muhammad frowned. Aaliyah tried not to smile.

"He saved my life," Viviana said, surprising him. "But he's still a shithead."

Muhammad's face colored. "I am here, just so the two of you are aware!"

His wife and mother ignored him. He didn't know if he should feel insulted or amused.

"I have no purpose left," Jamila said, finally looking away from the window. Her gaze settled on Viviana's profile. "I'm a useless old woman whose husband is dead, whose looks have long since faded, and who will be entirely alone when my Aaliyah takes a husband."

"Ummi," Aaliyah breathed out, "I would never leave you to be alone, nor would Momo."

Muhammad was stunned. He felt more than a little sick inside that his mother believed as she did while he'd been too busy to notice.

Viviana's head turned. Her heart was in her eyes. "I am motherless. I need you as much as your children do."

Jamila started to sob, something he'd never seen his mother do. Viviana undid her seatbelt and before he knew it the two women were hugging.

Muhammad and Aaliyah glanced at each other, both of their expressions asking the other what they should do or say. Eventually his sister shrugged, providing "Sheikh Shithead" no glimpse into the female psyche at all. He grunted.

"Momo," his mother chastised while hugging his wife, "such sounds are not becoming of the ruler of Raqqah."

He sighed, the sound that of a longsuffering man. His sister, brat that she was, looked away, assuming wrongly he couldn't see her grin.

"You're still quite beautiful," Viviana assured his mother. "The only difference between you and every other widow your age is you have an actual natural beauty as opposed to one painted on with a butter knife."

"Do you think so?" Jamila asked hopefully.

"I've been telling you that for years, ummi," Aaliyah interjected. "You just chose not to believe me."

Viviana smiled, first at his sister and then at his mother. "You see? You could totally remarry if you chose to."

"My father might not appreciate that!" Muhammad snapped.

His wife chose that moment to finally look at him, albeit with narrowed eyes. He'd take what he could get.

"According to you and your religion, he's in paradise with seventy-two virgins. He'll get over it."

Muhammad's nostrils flared. "Is that what you are hoping for, Viviana? That I die so you are free to remarry?"

"Momo," his mother said, affronted, "you shouldn't make everything about you."

"Really," Viviana seconded.

"I'm happy everyone is bonding at my expense!" He angrily slashed a hand through the air. "We are preparing to land in Dubai and switch to a smaller plane on the tarmac. If you are a woman, put on a damn hijab!"

If Muhammad thought the flight from Damascus to Dubai was tense, the flight from Dubai to the eighth emirate of Raqqah was the very definition of edgy. Now even his sister wasn't speaking to him. In fact the only one talking to him at all was Viviana—if he could call reverting back into that damn caricature of a Muslim wife talking.

He hated those fake smiles and even faker, exaggerated gestures of humility and obedience. He knew what all three of them were doing and he refused to succumb.

"Oh all right!" Muhammad fumed, succumbing. "Ummi, you may remarry if you so desire!"

At last his mother looked at him. She smiled. "You're a good son. I don't know that I wish to, but it's nice to know the option is available to me."

He grunted. His sister smiled at him so he grunted again.

Now it was Muhammad whose arms were folded across his chest. He sat there and stared at Viviana, waiting for her to act like her usual bitchy self. He didn't have to wait long.

"You see how easy it is to get along when you don't order people around *and tell them what to do even when they are in the right?*" she asked pointedly. He knew Viviana was referring to his idiotic comment about her rude behavior. "And by the way? If you ever take a second wife I am so out of here." She splayed her hands. "Let's just get that out of the way now."

Jamila nodded. "Begin as you mean to go on, daughter."

"Agreed," his traitor of a sister piped in. "And I want it in whatever marriage contract you sign on my behalf that my marriage is annulled if the man who is to be my husband ever takes another wife."

Muhammad was too busy staring at *his* wife to answer that with more than a grunt of accession. Viviana had, however unwittingly, shown jealousy and possessiveness toward him he hadn't known she felt. It wasn't everything, but it was a damn good start. It gave him hope that there could be happiness between them over the long haul.

"I can barely handle *you*," Muhammad barked at his wife. "The last time I was given no choice because my father insisted I wed them both for political reasons. Now *I* am the Shithead Sheikh in charge and I already married who I desired!"

All three women burst into laughter. Muhammad frowned at them.

He couldn't wait to reach his palace in Raqqah. A glass of wine was calling to him.

## Chapter Nine

Viviana spent hours touring the palace and grounds. The estate was massive, perched on approximately twelve hectares of grassy alcoves and sandy beach. Mature fruit trees were in abundance, growing everything from bananas, olives, dates, and figs to fruits she suspected had been imported, such as apples, oranges, and mangos.

It was truly a desert oasis, complete with its own private beach on the Persian Gulf. The palace itself gave off an "Old Arabia meets modern influences" kind of feel. Blending in with its natural surroundings, the hue of the exterior walls shifted in color with the position of the sun. She had taken the time to look around the fortress's lavish inside first, but it was the simplistic outside, specifically the view of the Gulf from the date tree she sat under, that was already her favorite place. Viviana absently toyed with the *mahr* necklace she wore as she stared at the orange-red sun preparing to dip behind the vast blue waters and sleep for the night.

"It's beautiful, is it not."

She hadn't heard Muhammad approach. Viviana replied, even though his question had been asked like a statement. "Yes. It truly is."

He sat down beside her and held out an open palm. Two plump dates sat inside his cupped hand. "Thank you." She took one and popped it into her mouth. "These are even sweeter than the ones in Syria."

Muhammad was quiet for a long moment. Viviana assumed he was simply watching the sun set as she was.

"I told you your *mahr* would come in two parts," he said, snagging her attention.

"That's right, you did." Her forehead crinkled as she regarded him. She had forgotten that until he'd reminded her just now. "What was the second part?"

"Information."

"Information?"

"Naam." *Yes.*

"What kind of information?"

Muhammad handed her an envelope. "This wasn't easy to procure and it took me all this time to do so." He stood up. "I hope it gives you the peace you seek."

Viviana's eyebrows knit together as she watched him walk toward the palace. When he was out of sight, she turned back toward the setting sun and opened the envelope. The contents made her hands tremble.

"General Qabbani,"she said aloud, her nostrils flaring. The same asshole that had raided the CIA installation three years past. The same monster responsible for the rapes and deaths of so many of her female colleagues. The brutal sadist who'd ordered the beheadings of several male co-workers on live television. The sick fuck that had enslaved Marisol, Kendra, Michaela, and Marie…

Viviana shook with a tumultuous mix of rage and heartache. It had taken over five years to acquire the name of the devil responsible for the murder of her parents, but now she had it. General Qabbani.

\* \* \* \* \*

Muhammad heard Viviana enter their apartments, but didn't glance up. He doubted possessing the knowledge of who had killed her parents would bring her peace, but hopefully at least his wife could find some semblance of closure.

"He is a sick demon who doesn't deserve to be alive."

Muhammad smiled without humor as he sipped from his glass of red, Parisian wine. He didn't pretend not to know exactly whom Viviana was talking about. "Do you wish to be his executioner?"

"Yes. No. I don't know." She sighed as she took a seat at the table opposite him. "I'm not like him."

"I'm aware. I wouldn't have married you otherwise." Muhammad set down his glass. "You needn't worry, *hayati*. Qabbani no longer has the luxury of breathing. Would you care for some wine?"

"Did you kill him? And yes please." He could see Viviana glancing around their apartments. She probably wondered why the ones they'd just left behind in Damascus had been built and decorated so similarly. "This is nice. You never have to feel away from home when you're in Syria."

His eyebrows rose. She was the first person to ever arrive at the correct conclusion without any help. Even his sister, who Muhammad was so close to, had questioned him. "Astute observation," he murmured, handing her a glass of red wine. "And no, I didn't have anything to do with Qabbani's death. His own soldiers saw to that."

She muttered something under her breath. At his quizzical expression, she said louder, "They are as sadistic as he is."

"Many, but fortunately not most. Hence his death."

Viviana nodded. Silence ensued as they sipped from their wine glasses. Her expression was contemplative. Muhammad wanted to know what she was thinking, but decided it would be prudent to give her time to process everything.

"It doesn't help," she finally said, her voice quivering a bit. "I thought knowing would help, but it really doesn't."

"I know," he said quietly. "Because it doesn't bring them back."

A single tear tracked down her cheek as her gaze found his. "Yet you acquired the information anyway because you realized from firsthand experience I couldn't know having the answer wouldn't help until I had it."

"Something like that," he murmured.

Viviana stared at him in silence. Muhammad couldn't be sure what direction her thoughts were going in.

"Why?" she asked softly. At his confused look, she clarified, "Why did you do this for me? And why did you negotiate for me? Who did you negotiate for me with and what did they get out of it?"

"Be certain you genuinely want the answers before you ask the questions."

Her teeth sank into her bottom lip. She mulled that over for a suspended pause.

"Tell me," she whispered.

Muhammad took a deep breath and slowly expelled it. "I acquired the information for you because I know how it feels to lose your family in such a brutal, unnecessary way." He reached up to his head and absently pulled off the red and white checkered *kufiya* scarf he wore. "I obtained the information for you because I realized you could never find a sense of closure without it."

"And the rest?"

This was going to be difficult. Both to tell and to hear.

"Your people," he quietly admitted. "I negotiated with your own people."

Viviana sat stoically, her expression indecipherable. Muhammad said nothing, just continued to stare at her.

"My government planned the deaths of four of its own soldiers and three of its CIA agents?" Her laugh was humorless. "So the world would blame al-Baghdadi for it, I presume?"

He inclined his head. "Naam."

"Why did they let me live?" she ground out. "Why me?"

"Because I gave them my word you would never be heard from again if they let me keep you."

"I see." Viviana's crimson fingernails began tapping on the table. "Why did they beat you? For effect?"

Muhammad waved that away. "Those ones knew nothing. They were vicious for the sake of being vicious."

"Apparently a trait they gleaned from their master."

"Touché."

"How high up did this go?" Her face blanched. "The president I voted for?"

"I doubt it," Muhammad answered honestly. "In case you didn't notice, the CIA tends to operate all on its own."

His poor wife looked as relieved as she was sad and angry. "I still don't understand how you factor into all of this. I admit I never paid much attention to the intel that crossed my desk, but you've been the topic of more than one debriefing at headquarters. There's a bounty on your head."

"That story made it easier for al-Baghdadi to trust me."

"So that was a lie too? You are not Daesh?"

Muhammad couldn't help but frown. "Would we be drinking wine together if I was Daesh? Would you be permitted to ask me questions or walk around not dressed like a bloody beekeeper if I was Daesh?"

Viviana must have remembered the hijab she'd had to don when changing planes. She reached up and tugged it off. "I understand why you must loathe al-Baghdadi. Most Muslims do..."

"But?"

She sighed. "Surely you don't need the United States to get rid of him. Why haven't the Arab nations taken him out?"

"Getting them to agree on anything is as fruitless and disgruntling as waiting for your Democrats and Republicans to hold hands and skip through a meadow together."

"Point taken," she muttered.

"I took matters into my own hands. Nobody besides you realizes this."

Her eyes widened. "Aaliyah?"

"Laa." *No.* "She knows bits and pieces, but not much."

Silence engulfed the room. Muhammad stood up, suddenly desperate to be alone for a while. He walked toward the doors, pausing as he reached them. He spoke without looking back at her. "You can never leave me without being exterminated by your own people. You being freed of me is a risk they will not take."

"There's something you're not telling me," Viviana said quietly. "I can feel it."

Every muscle in Muhammad's body corded and tensed. Still, he didn't look back. "I haven't given you enough?"

"Not if it isn't everything."

He was uncommunicative for a drawn out moment, not wanting to "go there" as his wife would call it. In the end, he acquiesced. He turned around to face her.

"I lied to you once. Only once, but still I lied."

Viviana said nothing, only listened. Muhammad continued.

"I am not a fan or champion of your country's interfering ways," he said simply. "I do not trust your government any more than I trust al-Baghdadi's."

"Go on," she murmured.

"I helped them for one reason and one reason only— revenge."

She gently shook her head. "I don't understand."

"When my family was murdered in the drone strike, al-Baghdadi blamed it on the United States in order to gain my loyalty and financial backing. Later, I found out the man who calls himself caliph had ordered the air raid."

Viviana's eyes widened. Her jaw dropped open a bit.

"I lied when I said you must give me six children to make up for the three your people killed," Muhammad admitted. "al-Baghdadi murdered them for the same reason your government thought to murder you."

"Collateral damage," she whispered, her eyes unblinking.

"Collateral damage," Muhammad softly confirmed.

Her heart was in her downcast gaze. Unable to bear not knowing what she now thought of him, Muhammad turned and exited their apartments.

* * * * *

It was an overwhelming amount of information to absorb and soul-crushing knowledge just to be cognizant of. Viviana didn't doubt the truth behind Muhammad's confessions...she just wasn't altogether certain how to process them. Had she been a civilian who'd never seen firsthand the sorts of barbarisms her government—hell *any* government—was capable of, his tale would have been difficult to credit. Unfortunately and fortunately, she wasn't. Muhammad's words had merely caused the pieces of the puzzle to click together and form a coherent picture for her.

Letting her body sink into the warm water of the bathing pool, Viviana didn't hear Muhammad's return. She stayed submerged as long as she was able, the inviting bathwater relaxing her tense muscles. Broaching the surface when she needed some air, Viviana kept her eyes closed as she took in a large gulp and forced her body to sink back down under the liquid as far as possible. She bobbed back up quicker than she would have liked.

"My fucking tits and ass," Viviana muttered to herself. "Have to make it impossible for me to stay under, don't you?"

"I love your big tits and ass."

Viviana screamed. She instinctively splashed water at Muhammad and threw a sponge at him. "Oh my God," she squeaked. "You scared me to death!"

He was dressed only in serwal pajama pants, which fell below his navel. His happy trail had grown in, which she found sexy. Apparently he'd been too preoccupied to shave lately.

Muhammad squatted down on his thighs. "What was the sponge going to do if I had been an intruder?"

Viviana gave him a *ha-ha-ha* look. "Clean you to death maybe?"

He grinned. "I need a reason to be dirty first."

"Hmmm…"

Jamila and Aaliyah burst into the room. Aaliyah was wielding a knife and her mother a semi-automatic weapon. "What has happened?" they screeched in unison, both of them wide-eyed and disheveled.

Viviana's lips formed an O. Muhammad grunted.

"I scared her by accident," he informed the duo. "But thank you for protecting her, Rambo and Crocodile Dundee."

Jamila let out a sigh. "Why do you upset your mother so? It's one o'clock in the morning, Muhammad. Your sister and I heard your wife's scream all the way from the west wing. Have I not taught you it is impolite and ungentlemanly to scare a woman?"

Viviana covered her smile with a pretend yawn. Muhammad wore the expression of a sheikh too exhausted to argue with his mother.

"Naam, ummi," Muhammad mumbled. He sounded more the obedient five-year-old son than the ruler of a sheikhdom. "My apologies."

"Vivi," a sleepy but armed Aaliyah called out.

"Naam?"

"Have you eaten?"

"Laa." *No.* She sighed. "I was preoccupied."

"I will stop in the kitchens on my way back to bed and have a food trolley sent down."

Viviana smiled. "Shukran." *Thank you.*

"Have them leave it outside the door," Muhammad instructed. "She is still bathing."

"I'm tired, not blind, Momo." Aaliyah shook her head and smiled. "Let's go, ummi. No gunning down madmen tonight. Maybe tomorrow."

"Goodnight, daughter," Jamila said to Viviana. "And goodnight to my son who's lucky my eyesight is better than my aim."

"Goodnight," Viviana and Muhammad said in unison.

# Chapter Ten

Now that his mother and sister were gone, Muhammad went back to giving his wife his full attention. *Wallah,* she was the most beautiful woman inside and out. He wanted to ask her how she felt about him now that she was aware he had told her that one lie, but she was still grinning from the scene his family had made.

"Back before I liked your mom..." Viviana began.

"Twelve hours ago?" Muhammad mused.

"Yeah, then." Viviana's smile kicked up. "I used to call her Jamila-the-Hun in my head. Now I will call her that anyway, but for a different reason."

Muhammad chuckled. "She will take pride in that name."

"I do not doubt that."

His expression grew serious as he stared at his gorgeous, naked wife. She wore nothing but her *mahr* necklace, which dangled provocatively between her ripe, wet breasts. Her dark gold curls, still drenched, had been straightened by the weight of the water. Her eye makeup had partially come off, giving Viviana what she likely would have thought were raccoon eyes, but which Muhammad thought added to her sultry, exotic appeal. The smudged kohl made her light eyes sparkle, giving him an erection.

"Finish your bath," Muhammad murmured. He reclined on his right side next to the bathing pool, propped up by his elbow. "I am content just to watch you."

"Maybe I'm not content," Viviana returned.

Her words stung, but he said nothing. He couldn't blame her for not trusting him after he'd lied to her. It hurt, but—

"Maybe I won't be content until I see where this leads to."

Muhammad's eyes widened as his wife's index finger found his navel and slowly trailed down the line of hair leading to his cock. He sucked in his breath, the competing feelings of confusion, arousal, and embarrassment at war inside him. Was she teasing him as punishment? Was she pointing out his body hair was *haram*—forbidden—to shame him?

"I'm sorry I forgot to shave." His face flushed. "I'm an Arab. It grows back too fast."

Viviana's gaze narrowed in what looked to be…hell, he didn't know anymore.

"Do you have to shave it?" his wife whispered. "It turns me on."

His embarrassment grew. "You are saying that to punish me. I am sorry I lied to you, Viviana. I will never lie again. I promise I—"

"Punish you?" She sighed as she continued to run her finger over his line of hair. "Muhammad, I would not tell you this happy trail turns me on if it didn't. And I don't think you need punished because you didn't lie—not really. Side A strikes, Side B retaliates, Side A strikes back, Side B retaliates. At the end of the day…" She shrugged. "I can't tell Side A from Side B anymore."

Now he felt even guiltier. She was too kind and forgiving. She must have seen the culpability in his expression.

"You're not going to let this go until I'm mad at you for real, are you?"

His appearance was grim. "Probably not."

She half snorted and half laughed. "Okay fine. I'm mad." Her finger trailed down his line of hair again, this time disappearing into the serwal pajama pants he wore. She grabbed his stiff cock and squeezed it. He hissed. "Your punishment is to not shave that happy trail *ever*." She pulled his cock out. "Or any of the things it leads to."

He had forgotten that non-Muslim men didn't make a habit of shaving off all their body hair, but then it was easy to forget Viviana wasn't Arab-born for her accent was that of a native speaker's. His embarrassment vanished, replaced by total arousal. If she liked the "happy trail" then it would remain.

All higher thought deserted Muhammad as his wife took his cock into her mouth. She stood at the bathing pool's edge, her full lips wrapping around his erection. She closed her eyes and sucked his cock with an expression that told him she loved doing this to him.

Viviana picked up the pace, her head bobbing up and down as she moaned around his rigid cock. Muhammad wrapped his left hand around the back of her head, groaning as she sucked him in fast, deep strokes. The sound of suctioning lips meeting firm flesh reverberated throughout the room.

He had always wondered what a blowjob felt like for it was a sexual act his deceased wives had not performed on him. The reality of this was better than all the thousands of his fantasies combined. And to have it performed by her, his wife, the woman of his dreams...

Viviana sucked his cock faster and faster, her head bobbing at an animalistic pace. Muhammad's jaw clenched as she kept up the frenetic speed, her mouth sucking and sucking and sucking. He wanted the moment to last forever, but his arousal was too great. She took him deeper into her throat, still lapping him up in frenzied motions.

He came on a bellow, his orgasm powerful enough to force his torso to spasm a bit. And still she kept suckling from him, her lips latched around his cock, her throat swallowing his still spurting cum.

"I think I gave you a liter," Muhammad rasped, his breathing heavy. "*Wallahhhh.*"

When Viviana was finished extracting every drop he had to give, she unlatched her puffy lips from his semi-flaccid cock with a pop. She grinned.

Muhammad smiled as best he could for a man who could barely recall his own name at the moment. "I'm rolling into the pool," he warned her, panting, "So you might wish to back up a bit."

She laughed as he did just that, his big body causing a decently sized splash.

* * * * *

Their bath had taken much longer than planned, but then he hadn't expected his wife to want more sex. It was good he had paid the extra *dirham* for the self-cleaning bathing pool.

Even now as they sat at the table, naked and eating, he could hear the mechanism working overtime to make the basin *halal* again. He had a feeling he would finally get his money's worth out of the self-cleaner. Viviana loved the water as much as she loved fucking him in it.

"Tell me your thoughts," Muhammad said, stabbing his Fattoush salad with a fork.

Viviana swallowed the bite in her mouth. "Well for starters, you make this salad much better than whoever prepared this one. It's still good, it's just not great."

Her compliment pleased him. He couldn't help but crack a small smile. "Thank you, Skeikha al-Raqqah."

She grinned. "No Sheikha Shithead?"

"Not tonight. Maybe tomorrow."

Her smile slowly faded. "It isn't right, Muhammad." At his inquiring expression she clarified, "They shouldn't get away with what they've done. I might not have been best friends with my housemates and colleagues, but I knew them well enough to know they were good people, all of them performing their jobs out of patriotism. Patriotism I now question the validity of," she muttered, "but patriotism nevertheless." She shook her head slightly. "The American people deserve better than this—they deserve to know the truth."

There wasn't much he could say to that so he grunted his agreement. "The sad part is it's what ninety-nine percent of the planet does," he sighed. "Perform their duty out of loyalty, I mean."

Now it was Viviana who grunted. "Hashtag Truth." Her eyes narrowed. "I thought about uploading a video to YouTube and telling the world what was done to me and my colleagues, but it wouldn't do any good. They'd just spin-doctor it and make me come across as the brainwashed wife of a terrorist."

Muhammad stilled. He set down his fork as he remembered something.

"What?" Viviana asked. "What is it?"

He blinked. "I was in such a hurry to leave Syria that I forgot the video footage I left behind. Fuck!"

"Footage of whaaaa—oh dang… me masturbating?"

He couldn't help but chuckle. "That too." At her mortified expression, he added, "It's hidden and will not be found unless I retrieve it myself."

"Phew. That could have been embarrassing."

"al-Baghdadi must know by now that I'm aware of what he did—and that I have taken my revenge. If that's the case, the house we left has likely been burned to the ground. Then again, he was never the sharpest tool in the shed."

Viviana filled their wine glasses. She handed him one. "Whatever footage you have hidden there isn't worth a beheading." Her expression grew contemplative. "What were you doing in Syria anyway? I mean, if you're from the Emirates, why keep a palace in Damascus?"

"My father, the former sheikh of Raqqah, is from the Emirates. My mother is Syrian-born." Muhammad shrugged. "He loved her dearly so he had a palace built there for her."

"That's sweet. No wonder she still mourns him."

"I have to go back," Muhammad said. "I need—we need—that footage."

Her aqua eyes rounded. "No way! Like I said, whatever video you have there isn't worth the possible consequence of attempting to retrieve it."

"It has everything you need for a video that can't be spin-doctored."

"I don't care! The answer is no!"

His eyebrows slowly drew together. "Is that a hint of caring I detect from my wife who only refers to me as her husband when forced?"

Viviana's face flushed. "*Yesss*," she hissed. "Yes it is!"

His expression softened. "I am a highly skilled warrior, Viviana. I will know if I need to retreat."

She sighed. "I can already tell I won't be able to talk you out of this." She picked up a napkin and threw it at him. "You can't just do things like this, everybody else's feelings be damned!"

"Why do you care?" Muhammad prodded.

He'd backed her into a corner and they both knew it. She stubbornly refused to speak.

"Why?" he murmured.

Her jaw tightened. "Because I love my husband," she bit out.

His smile was so wide it caused a bit of pain at the sides of his lips. "Was that so difficult to admit?" He waved his hand. "Never mind. Of course it was."

Viviana did her cute little snort-laugh. "Well it's out there now."

"You must tell me this every day."

"Then you must stay here, far away from Syria."

His expression grew solemn. "Vivi, the more I think on it the more I realize I have to. You were right—Americans do deserve to know. The whole world deserves to know for that matter."

Her expression was desperate. "I changed my mind."

Muhammad reached out and gently placed his hand over hers. "For your safety. For my mother and sister's safety. For the safety of any child you give me—inshallah." *God willing.* "I must."

It took Viviana a long moment to succumb, but she did. "You better come back here alive and you better not be gone long." She removed her hand from under his, picked up her fork, and resumed eating. "And just so you know? I have a feeling the child you want is already a done deal."

If his smile was huge before, it was over the moon now. "Really?"

"Wallah." *I swear to God.*

Thinking clearly, Muhammad frowned thoughtfully. "No more wine then."

Viviana's head shot up. "Oh shit! What if I've caused something bad—"

"You haven't." He shook his head and smiled. "We have never drank more than a glass maybe twice a week. Sometimes not that much."

"Are you quitting while I have to?"

"Of course."

"Are you coming back to us alive?"

"Of course."

"Promise?"

Muhammad's eyes sparkled. Nothing in this world or any other could keep him away. He hadn't known true love and complete fulfillment until he'd known Viviana. *"Wallah."*

# Epilogue
*One Year Later*

Muhammad sat next to his wife on the sofa, grinning as he bounced their five-month-old daughter on his knee. Ensconced in the palace's communal living room, a place where the entire family could spend time together, Viviana grumbled that she couldn't figure out the remote to the new theater quality television he'd purchased.

"I couldn't either." His mother threw her hands up. "Nor could Aaliyah. Momo, give me Darya so you can fix this."

"I just got her," he said, keeping his voice as happy as his face. Darya was giggling and he didn't want her to stop. "I can never pry her from your hands, ummi."

Viviana smiled. She leaned in closer and kissed their daughter on the nose. "Such a happy baby," his wife cooed. "Ummi's happy girl."

Muhammad's trusted servant Hani appeared. He cleared his throat. "My apologies, Sheikh. Sheikha, you have visitors."

All three women who bore the title looked at Hani. He could have sworn even the tiny sheikha on his lap glanced over.

Hani's face flushed. "Sheikha Viviana."

"Me?" Viviana asked, puzzled.

"Naam."

She sighed. "Is it someone I need to put a hijab on for?"

"There is a male with a female."

Viviana looked at Muhammad. His eyes narrowed thoughtfully. Why would a man and a woman come here to speak to her? His wife had turned out to be quite the homebody so she didn't venture into the cities often. Whenever she did, it was usually with him. "Put it on until we know who it is," he muttered. "The same for the rest of you."

His wife had made it clear a long time ago that if he wanted servants in the house then he better not mind them seeing her hair. As a consequence, he employed only men who had been exceedingly loyal to him and his father before him. He would take no chances with gossipy types — it would cause quite a stir if his people knew he permitted the women in his household to reveal their hair to male servants. Not that the servants gazed at their hair overly long. They'd gotten that out of their system within a week or so.

"It looks like you get your wish, ummi," Muhammad said, standing. He kissed Darya's sweet head. "I will bring her to —"

"I'll take her!" Aaliyah interrupted. She jumped to her feet, much quicker at wrapping her hair than their mother. "My niece adores her auntie."

It was a wonder Muhammad ever got to hold his daughter at all. If she wasn't nursing at his wife's breast, his mother and sister were quick to claim her. Not that he would complain. He couldn't have been blessed with a happier life. He winked at Aaliyah as he handed the baby over.

It was his sister who had first suggested to Muhammad and Viviana that they name their daughter Darya. In Arabic, her moniker meant *sea* — the color of eyes she shared with her mother. His wife had loved the name, as had he, and so the youngest Sheikha of Raqqah had been christened thusly.

"I believe we're ready, Hani," Viviana said. She smoothed out her kaftan. "You can show them in."

Hani inclined his head and retreated. Muhammad stood next to his wife even though he was aware the visitors would have already been scanned for gunpowder residue, patted down, and checked for weapons again by x-ray before nearing the front doors. The sheikh took every precaution these days, the thought of losing his wife and daughter too desolate to contemplate.

143

Within a few minutes Hani returned with the mystery guests in tow. An Arab man as tall and muscular as Muhammad stood next to a woman wearing the beekeeper's dress—a black burka that covered even her eyes. The male looked to be in his late thirties. The woman's age was anyone's guess.

"Sheikha Viviana al-Raqqah?" the man asked.

"Naam," Muhammad interrupted, speaking for her. He crossed his arms over his chest. He wasn't normally so overtly territorial, but then he wasn't accustomed to a strange man smiling at his wife. He decided he didn't like it. Especially when the strange man's physical attractiveness rivaled his own, he conceded, frowning. "The sheikha is my wife. Who the hell are you?"

"Muhammad!" Viviana whispered harshly. Her eyes widened in embarrassment. "Hashtag WTF?"

"My apologies, Sheikh Muhammad," the man said, his smile never faltering. "I am Aariz. My wife and I have travelled far to see the sheikha. I was uncertain of your customs so she donned the burka to cover all bases. May she remove it?"

"Of course," Viviana said. She elbowed Muhammad in the ribs. "Right?"

He cleared his throat and found his manners. "Yes, of course."

"My husband gets a little grouchy when he hasn't had his dinner yet," Viviana lied as the woman slowly removed her veil. "You'll have to forgive him."

Muhammad grunted. "I'm not a gremlin."

"Okay that doesn't even make sense," his wife huffed. "Gremlins don't become gremlins unless they are fed after midnight." She splayed her hands. "I don't see how..." Viviana's voice trailed off as Aariz's wife removed her veil. "Oh my God," she breathed out.

Muhammad's forehead wrinkled. "Do you know her?"

It was as if she couldn't hear him. "You're alive," Viviana whispered. He could feel her body trembling even as her lips curved into a smile. "You're alive!"

He watched in confusion as the two women threw themselves at each other, both of them hugging and crying. They talked animatedly in such rapid English that he could scarcely understand it. Glancing at Aariz, the other man's shrug told him he wasn't the only one having trouble following.

"What has happened?" Muhammad's mother asked, coming to stand next to him. Praise be to Allah for her interference! At least this once. "Viviana? Who is this?"

Viviana released her hold on the mystery woman and swiped at her tears. "Jamila—I'm sorry—I..."

His mother quickly walked to wear Viviana stood. "Shh shh," she said soothingly. "There is no need to apologize. Perhaps we should all sit down and talk?"

Viviana nodded. At last his wife glanced at him, smiling through her tears. He was too concerned to smile, but he realized she was a master at reading his gaze. She knew he was worried.

"I don't know any more than you do," Aariz said under his breath as they walked into the dining room. "My wife insisted on coming here after seeing you and the sheikha on YouTube and then again on Al-Jazeera. She said everything would be explained when we got here."

"That's good to know," Muhammad muttered, "because my curiosity is killing me."

"It's the same for me. *Wallah*."

It took another five minutes for everyone to be seated, then another few minutes more to get a coherent answer, but eventually Muhammad and Aariz were rewarded for their patience. They both listened to their wives' stories as wide-eyed as his mother and sister were.

"It was Marisol who was in that closet with me," Viviana said, shaking. "When they tore her out of the closet and stripped her naked, I just — oh my God."

"They *what*?" Aariz growled.

"It's okay, babe," Marisol said, smiling. "You of all people know I escaped."

"I've been hating myself for three years," Viviana gasped, tears streaming down her face. She grabbed Marisol's hands and squeezed. "I should have done something or — "

"There was nothing you could have done, Vivi. *Nothing*." Marisol's expression broached no argument. "We were the last two survivors who hadn't been taken. We had no weapons and they had an arsenal!"

"Oh my God," Aaliyah whispered. "You have both lived through nightmares."

Muhammad put a hand on his wife's shoulder and gently squeezed. He had known she was the one who got away, but she had never detailed the events leading up to it for him. Realizing the subject to be a sensitive one for Viviana, he had never pressed the issue. Now his heart felt broken for her. He understood too well the horror it was to live with survivor's guilt. Later, when they were alone, they would talk through this.

"Do you know what became of the other three pretty girls?" his mother asked.

Marisol shook her head. "I was hoping Vivi knew." Her smile was sad. "Maybe now that Muhammad and Vivi are headline news the world over..." She sighed. "I pray they come here to Raqqah as I did. If they are alive and able to, I know they will."

"Kendra has the best odds of survival," Viviana said thoughtfully. "She was trained to be—"

"An efficient killer," Marisol finished.

His wife nodded. "She was—is—an expert assassin. That information wouldn't have been in the files General Qabbani got his hands on." Viviana's eyes sparkled. "I always wondered how they'd found her, much less taken her. Now I wonder if Kendra wasn't just biding her time and calculating the odds of when and where to strike."

"I hope you're right," Marisol sighed. "I really do."

After another thirty minutes or so the reunited women switched to a happy topic. Muhammad was never so relieved to let a subject drop. Every word his wife had spoken while reliving the past had broken his heart for her all over again.

But their beautiful daughter? He could discuss his little sheikha until the end of days.

"Naam," Muhammad said to Aariz, smiling as he bounced her on his knee, "Darya is our first. How many do you and Marisol have?"

"Two. They are at home with my ummi." Aariz did what all proud daddies do and pulled their photos from his wallet. "One daughter and one son." He grinned. "My daughter has the temper of her mother. My son takes after me."

"They're gorgeous!" Viviana said, looking at the photos with Muhammad. "How did you two meet anyway?"

The couple looked at each other and shared a smile. "It's a long story," they said in unison.

"Then I'm glad you are staying through the weekend," Viviana replied, grinning. "I can tell by the look you gave each other it's worth hearing."

\* \* \* \* \*

His exhausted wife had fallen asleep as soon as Darya finished nursing. Muhammad had shooed Viviana off to bed before tending to their daughter. Burped, nappy changed, and sound asleep in her crib, he walked to their bed and stretched out next to his wife. She instinctively curled up against him as she always did, burrowing into his side. He kissed her forehead.

"I love you," Viviana sleepily whispered.

"I love you too, *hayati*," he murmured back.

"Thank you for being my husband."

He smiled. Even asleep she never forgot their ritual. "Thank you for being my wife."

Within seconds he heard her faint snoring. His smile widened.

Muhammad would never forget or stop missing his sons, but he could finally allow them to rest in peace with their mothers. It had taken time to come to terms with their losses, but Viviana had been there for him, helping him find his way, encouraging him to remember instead of trying to forget.

His sons lived on in Darya. The way she smiled, the shape of her nose, her adorable giggle...it was the little things that reminded him of the various traits she shared in common with her brothers. In Darya he could remember them, yet still see her for the unique, special gift that she was.

From the mutually experienced flames of bleakness and loss Allah had sent Muhammad and Viviana phoenixes of hope and joy in the form of each other—and then their daughter. Sheikh Muhammad al-Jihad al-Raqqah was a happy, fortunate man. He held on tightly to his wife, falling asleep to the familiar, comforting sound of her barely audible snore.

# Author's Notes

I took some artistic liberty with names and places. Here is my list of clarifications in no particular order:

1. Many Arab women do not take their husband's surname upon marriage. In some countries it is forbidden to do so. This tradition is observed to keep inbreeding from occurring. The prophet Muhammad was adamantly against marrying within one's family, which was an accepted norm in Arabia prior to the establishment of Islam. Before Muhammad came to power, sons routinely wed their mothers after their fathers passed on.

2. The United Arab Emirates consists of seven sheikhdoms, not eight.

3. Raqqah is not a part of the UAE, but is instead a city in Syria; it is now the de facto capitol of ISIS/ISIL.

4. Muhammad's surname could only be al-Raqqah if he had been born in and/or heralded from Raqqah, Syria.

5. I chose Raqqah (also spelled Raqqa) hoping it would make readers curious enough to google it and see the daily atrocities occurring there. It is my

hope that the suffering of the Syrian people becomes important to us all.

6. Recommended viewing: <u>Salam Neighbor</u> on Netflix.


Peace,

Jaid

Made in the USA
Middletown, DE
04 January 2019